Why so much fear of tears? Because the masks we use are made of salt. A stinging, red salt which makes us beautiful and majestic but devours our skin.
Luisa Valenzuela

OTHER TITLES IN THE *MASKS* SERIES

Neil Bartlett *Who Was That Man?*
Michael Bracewell *The Crypto-Amnesia Club*
Ian Breakwell *The Artist's Dream*
Gianni Celati *Voices From the Plains*
Daniel de Souza *Under a Crescent Moon*
Leslie Dick *Without Falling*
Janice Eidus *Faithful Rebecca*
Janice Eidus *Vito Loves Geraldine*
Alison Fell (ed.) *The Seven Deadly Sins*
Juan Goytisolo *Landscapes After the Battle*
Juan Goytisolo *Marks of Identity*
Steve Katz *Florry of Washington Heights*
Jonathan Lerner *Caught in a Still Place*
Raul Nuñez *The Lonely Hearts Club*
Luisa Valenzuela *The Lizard's Tail*

CAUGHT IN A STILL PLACE

CAUGHT IN A STILL PLACE

JONATHAN LERNER

The publishers thank Kathy Acker, Mark Ainley, Martin Chalmers, Bob Lumley, Enrico Palandri, Kate Pullinger, Antonio Sanchez for their advice and assistance.

British Library Cataloguing in Publication Data

Lerner, Jonathan
Caught in a still place.
I. Title II. Series
813'.54

ISBN 1-85242-146-0

First published 1989 by
Serpent's Tail, Unit 4, Blackstock Mews, London N4

Typeset by AKM Associates (UK) Ltd, Southall, London

Printed in Great Britain by
WBC Print (Bristol) Ltd

For Ellen

1

This morning, Jaydie noticed that the sun was coming up in a haze. She noticed it because it isn't normally humid down here in the winter. From Miss Audrey's house, at the highest point on Cape Harrier, where I've been living since Richard went away, we have a clear view east across the bay to the salt marsh and the pine and palmetto flats that stretch beyond it. As I say, it isn't damp here in the winter — even the swampy stands of cypress tend to dry out — and this year has been no exception. It has been on our minds, because it's a problem getting enough fresh water in a dry spell, ever since the pipeline from the mainland stopped flowing.

So when she heard me fixing breakfast, Jaydie came inside from where she had been pacing, on the porch, and mentioned it, about the haze. But I can't say we were surprised. There's nothing that normal, anymore.

After breakfast, I took Miss Audrey's elbow and helped her out to the porch. She seems to have a lot more trouble walking now. It could be arthritis, or I don't know what. During her occasional lapses into clarity she neglects to tell us what pains her. But actually she's had a stiff, rolling sort of walk as long as I've known her, as if her legs are hinged too far apart under her wide hips. "She walks like she's got a load in her pants," Richard muttered to me the first time we saw her coming our way, six or seven years ago.

I tucked Miss Audrey into her chair. Then I sat down on the porch floor, leaned back against the side of the house, and shut my eyes. The child had followed us out, silent as usual, and sat down next to me. It was cool this morning, but the porch faces south, and the sun was bright. This is how we spend the winter mornings, facing the sun to keep warm. Except for Jaydie, who has an internal generator that never stops cranking. "I'm going down to rinse these," she had said, as the rest of us were on our way outside. She gathered our bowls off the table and left through the kitchen door.

It must have been a pretty grand place when Miss Audrey's father built it as a summer cottage for his family — or was it her grandfather? She mixes things up now, and she's our only source. Twelve rooms, and the breezeway connecting the kitchen at the back. It's a once-white clapboard built up off the ground on brick piers, with a steep-pitched tin roof, made high like that to gather the heat in summer. Most of it has been shut up unused for years, and a long time ago, when they stopped cooking with wood, and living in terror of house fires, the back kitchen was abandoned and a room in the main house remodeled into one. Lucky for us, the old wood stove was never taken away. When we came to need it, after the electricity went dead for the last time and the propane truck had stopped making deliveries, the stove was waiting. We decided to bring it into the house, though, so we could use it for heat, too. We do need heat for a while in the winter. The thing weighed a fucking ton. Jaydie and me, pushing and shoving like a couple of mules. I guess that was the first time we did something really hard together, just us two.

From up here we have the best view. It's not a high hill, just the only one. To the east, there's the funnel-shaped bay, and two miles across it the flat mainland. To the south, the tip of Cape Harrier is arranged below us like the circle of a woman's full skirt, the ragged beach for its hem. On the bay side are a couple of docks that have collapsed. Near the southern point, up on pilings over the water, is the building where Bullie's bar used to be, and across the rutted street from it the old house where Richard and I ran an inn. The beach curves on around toward the Gulf, dotted with the shells of vacation homes, enclosing the scattered buildings and vacant lots of the little town.

It always was a small town — only a hundred and fifty people or so when Richard and I came, with a few dozen more on weekends — and isolated enough so that when things elsewhere started going really wrong it was hard for us to know it. They never had delivered a daily paper, so we couldn't read about it each morning, or notice when publication became erratic and finally ceased. The few latecomers to town, like Richard and me, or Jaydie and Bullie, had moved down here to get away. And the natives of the place — "Cape Harriettes" Richard liked to call them behind their backs — if they had stayed on into adulthood, seemed to be content enough in this miniature world rimmed by palmetto scrub and the sea.

So the decline was only shown to us in subtle absences, which in the languor of this place raised small concern, at least in the beginning. Weekend people came less and less frequently, and guests to the inn. The mail truck stopped arriving regularly, and the grocery truck, and the power started going off for periods that stretched into days and then weeks, and finally it, and the phones, went dead for good. Broadcast reception had always been chancy out here. Nobody had a satellite dish. Those who tried to tune in, picked up garbled, contradictory bits of news, or nothing.

Some people left, uneasy, seeking normalcy. For most of us — those like me who came for the peace, or the fishing folk who were used to a subsistence life anyway — things hadn't changed all that much. There were still more than a hundred people here when the sickness came. A hundred people, but no doctor or nurse or clue to what it was, just those who got sick and died real fast and the rest of us who somehow didn't. It was hideous to watch. Their skin just dissolved, fell away in patches. The bare flesh grew inflamed, putrefied. Each of them flared out in a red aura of fever.

Almost all the survivors left here in a panic. By then it would have taken an act of will to expect things would be all right somewhere else. It was just desperation to get away from this scene of horror. They went by rowboat up the river, or on foot — it had been a long time since there had been any gas. Once in a while now somebody shows up here, walking up the road, or sailing in, like an apparition, from the sea. But none of the people who left ever returned.

And at the moment, the town is empty, just the four of us up here on the hill, a couple of other straggler families on the far islands and in the woods. And all those useless cars with their shiny enamel bleaching dull in the relentless sun, smooth sheet metal slowly pitting from the blowing sand. You can see it all fine from here, because the porch runs across the whole south side of Miss Audrey's house.

If you go out the back, you see north, to where the cape protrudes from the mainland. To the right, the bay narrows into the muddy estuary of the river. Cape Harrier. Although that's a misnomer, I understand. For a while Richard decided he would become an expert on coastal geography. "It's not a cape," he announced one day, closing a book on his thumb. "It's a land-tied island. Built up over the years by sediment from the river." He turned to face the other islands that dot the mouth of the bay and protect us a little from the summer storms. "They all are, sedimentary. And also," he consulted his text again, "built up by sand dropped from the longshore current. The part that connects us to the mainland is called a tombolo." He meant the two-mile spit of sand running north toward the woods with the blacktop road on its back. It was flooded in the hurricane last summer and broken open in one place, making a new shallow pass into the bay. I guess we are no longer a land-tied island. I can't say why I remember all these terms. I'll lay odds Richard has forgotten them.

There was a light, steady breeze this morning, just enough to make the cabbage palms give off a silvery rustle and to sway the sheets of heavy plastic that Miss Audrey used to staple up across the east and south of the porch to protect her potted plants — staple up in the fall and pull down and roll up each spring, until the spring she didn't bother to pull them down again — ragged now after a couple of years' storms, gone brittle and burnished by the sun. For a while, I just sat there with my eyes closed, listening to the ends of the plastic scrape back and forth on the wooden floor, waiting to see if the morning would pass. Miss Audrey hummed the fragment of a blues, in a minor key.

"Mom," said the child quietly. I opened my eyes and saw her looking out where two sheets of plastic were parted by the breeze. She was looking at Jaydie, down by the water. Washing our breakfast dishes with handfuls of sand, I suppose, although I couldn't tell for sure. I'm near-sighted, and since my glasses got broken in a scuffle with Bullie last summer — no, that would have been the summer before — I've had to make do. I remembered what Jaydie had said about the haze at sunrise, and got up to have a look. It was another perfect, cloudless day, the sky a smooth china blue. Except down low in the east, where a brown smudge lay like a pencil mark.

Jaydie was swimming now, out in the bay, just a blob moving along the mirror sheen of the water, a rhythmic windmilling of arms. She swims the same way she paces, not for the exercise or because she loves the water, but to work something out of herself. This time of year the water is pretty chilly. I only go in to wash, normally. Almost high tide. At other times, the bay is so shallow you can walk across it knee deep. If you don't mind slicing your feet on oyster shells. I went back to my warm spot against the peeling clapboard.

"Mom," the child said a while later. Sometimes I think she hangs around me just to get on my nerves. But Jaydie was coming up the path, dripping wet, dishes in the crook of one arm and clothes in the other. She set everything down on the edge of the porch, and stood there.

I was pretty warm by this time and I tugged the sweater over my head. "Nice swim?" I asked.

"Julian," she said, in that tone she uses when she is introducing something we have to handle. "It's fire."

"What's fire?"

"It isn't fog, over there." She shrugged in the direction of the mainland. "I could smell it, when I was out in the bay. The woods are on fire."

I got to my feet. Not abruptly, though. I've been working on keeping my reactions calm. Alarm has not helped in any of the calamities so far. Miss Audrey appeared to be dozing.

Jaydie and I walked around to the east side of the house. The kid followed on our heels like a puppy. "See how it trails to the north?" Jaydie asked. "This wind is from the south. It's smoke."

It seemed very far away, but I know I'm not too good at judging distances. Still, I couldn't think of any difference it would make, anything we might do.

I decided that while the tide was in I would go after some wood. We've already cut and burned all the dead trees on the cape itself, and for a while we were ripping lumber off the more dilapidated houses. But that stuff burned up so fast it wasn't worth the effort of sawing it into pieces small enough to fit in the stove. So now we make wood runs in a rowboat, across to the mainland, or up the river, with an axe and a saw.

I'm not that good at handling a boat; Jaydie is. I asked

her how come one time, while we were paddling in the canoe out to the islands. I turned so I could look at her steering. But she didn't answer. I know she heard me. It was one of those silent, rippleless days on the water. But she just didn't answer. That's how she gets out of conversations she doesn't feel like getting into. She does it all the time.

I'll never forget the first time I saw her, across the bar in Bullie's. It was August. Bullie had all the jalousies opened and a hot dense wind came off the Gulf and blew through the room, carrying away the smoke from Richard's cigarette and from the stinking fat cigar that fat asshole Macnamara was chewing on. Macnamara was a legislator or a lobbyist or some kind of hustler who had built a vacation house here and used to come for long weekends eight months of the year from Montgomery or Tallahassee or wherever it was, a big sunburned jerk who didn't wear a shirt and laughed too loud at his own stories. He was in the middle of telling one to Bullie when Jaydie came in, the screen door springing shut behind her.

She ducked under the bar and went over to Bullie, slipping an arm around his narrow waist. They were living together then, in the apartment above the bar, which you reached by a wooden stairway that hung over the water. She just stood, while Macnamara went on with his guffawing. She had a bored air about her, looking at Macnamara without really watching him. She lit a cigarette after a while, and puffed at it while he talked, putting it between her lips and leaving it there and then raising her flat-open hand to take it out again between the second knuckles of two fingers. She reminded me of an Indian, with her high cheekbones and dark tan, but her hair was what used to be called dirty blonde when I was in high school. Maybe that's why I had this feeling I could picture her as she would have been in high school, fifteen or twenty years before. Tall, athletic for a girl, her hair thick and sleek. But I had the feeling she had had a hard time despite her good looks. She would have been handsome, not pretty, definitely not the cheerleader type. I was sure she had had to pay for that, and judging by the little creases in her face, I could see she had paid some in the years since, too. She wore two thick smears of green eyeshadow that afternoon in Bullie's but it didn't cover anything. I leaned over to Richard and said softly, under Macnamara's booming: "Don't you feel sometimes when you first lay eyes on somebody that you can tell exactly what they've had to go through in their life? Her." Richard glanced across at Jaydie, took a last drag, and stubbed out his Kool. "I wouldn't care to find out," he said, breathing out a lungful of smoke. Richard was like that.

She still looks pretty good, Jaydie, better maybe than in the years she was with Bullie. Things are so much simpler now. The skin on the bridge of her nose seems to be constantly peeling, and there's a copper-red cast to her suntan. She doesn't seem to care. None of us looks in mirrors anymore. And never mind trying to get Jaydie to put on a hat.

Rowing up the bay, the tide hadn't quite turned seaward, but still I sweated. I only had to go as far as the new pass that storm had cut. Jaydie and I brought a wheelbarrow over, afterwards, and we left it parked on its nose, the two handles sticking up into the air, at the far side, where the pavement picks up again more or less intact. Now when we go for wood, we walk it up the road into the woods. It's heavy when it's loaded, but one trip with a wheelbarrowful beats half a dozen with an armload. I guess all this is keeping me in shape. But I'm glad we are this far south and have these mild winters. I hate to think what's happened to people in places like Minnesota, or Quebec.

On my way back down the bay I could smell the fire all right. The little breeze had died away and the eastern sky was draped in a brown pall as the smoke drifted straight up, much closer now. It reminded me of mill pollution, and that reminded me of the invisible acrid pollution from the refineries along the river at Baton Rouge, which used to bother my eyes when I had my contacts in. I tied up at the dock, gathered an armful of wood, and walked up the hill.

Miss Audrey must have been inside. Jaydie was pushing the kid in the tire swing that hangs from the big oak in the corner of the yard. She was pushing her and talking to her, but she had her eyes across the bay. I asked if she wanted to help me carry the wood.

She didn't answer. She just kept pushing the swing, gazing up into the canopy of this tree which spreads so wide and holds up its own small forest. A carpet of ferns softens its dark trunk. In the crotch of two branches grows a prickly pear cactus, and saw palmettos are sprouting in the pockets of leaf debris trapped by other limbs. Silvery Spanish moss drapes the tree, and there are dense balls of mistletoe growing way up in its heights, globular and yellow-green as suns against the oak's own dusky olive foliage. This live oak is like an ark. It's home to squirrels and grackles and darting iridescent lizards. Sometimes I think it holds up the whole of living creation. Sometimes I feel that way myself. "Jaydie?" I prodded. I really wanted her help.

"You stay here, Sylvia," she told the child. She followed me down. I got into the boat and started handing up pieces of wood. She was kneeling on the dock, taking them and putting them into a pile.

All of a sudden she just sat down. "Juli, I'm scared," she said. This is a little game we play with each other.

"OK," I said, climbing out of the boat and sitting down cross-legged facing her. We held each other's hands and closed our eyes. "OK now."

"Julian, I'm scared," Jaydie began.

"Give it a name."

"The fire over there."

"Oh." It was my go. "Put a picture to it." How it works is we take turns describing what frightens us. I'm sure I wouldn't have been caught dead doing something like this before. I was never into the touchy-feely scene. It's surprising what adjustments you make.

Jaydie said, "Lots of chaos. Fire whipping through the woods. Everything bright orange. Lots of noise and a hot wind."

I thought for a minute. Up until now I hadn't been scared of the fire. I started wondering whether the woods would burn away. I wondered what we would do for firewood then. But this concern didn't seem quite on a level with Jaydie's images. "Pass," I said. "More?"

"Yeah. The animals. Armadillos caught in it, roasting. Wasted food. Alligators. Snakes."

"Roasting?"

"No. Alligators and snakes coming this way in front of the flames. Slithering, fast. Snakes swimming the bay."

I said, "Jaydie, I'm scared."

I had a feeling she opened her eyes for a second to look at me. "What do you see?" she asked.

"Snakes swimming across the bay. Cottonmouths. Tangles of them on the beach here, like spaghetti." There are certain crises we are simply not equipped to deal with, occurrences I try to avoid even imagining. Bad snake bites is one of them.

She squeezed my hands in hers. We sat there for a while. "More?" she asked.

"Yeah. No firewood. Freezing. Miss Audrey freezing."

"Wait a minute," she said. "I forget who started it."

"You did." That meant it was her go for the next question.

"OK. Who's got an answer?"

I tried to remember some old fragment of zoology. "Cold blooded animals can't sustain activity for very long."

"So what?"

"They slow down. Maybe they'll be too exhausted to swim across."

"Oh." I opened my eyes for a second and saw that she had hers open too, watching my face. That's not in the rules, but we're flexible with the rules. "I've got an answer for you, I think," she said.

"What?"

"Maybe the fire will stop when it reaches the river."

"So?"

"We can still cut firewood from the west bank."

Miss Audrey was sitting in her rocker when I got back

to the kitchen. "There's a fire over yonder in those woods," she announced. "Notice?" It was the first thing I'd heard her say all day. But she is usually more animated by this time of the afternoon. She perks up in time for supper. Sometimes she jabbers us crazy over the meal.

It was dark. Jaydie was outside on the porch. I could hear her regular footsteps on the hollow floor. It had started raining, or the palm fronds were scraping the side of the house in the wind. The two sounds, from inside, are identical. I figured it wasn't raining.

I had put Miss Audrey and Sylvia to bed. Jaydie and I each have a room to ourself, but those two sleep in the kitchen this time of year to be near the stove. With the way Miss Audrey smells — sour sometimes, chalky sometimes — and her sluggish frailty, and the fishy smells of much of what we cook, and the child's silent presence hovering and all the junk that collects in the kitchen, which is where we mainly live, it can get pretty close. Lucky for me there are all those other rooms, and all those other empty houses, when I need to get away.

Jaydie opened the door. "Julian," she said, peering around in the dark to see where I was. "Come out here a minute."

"The wind's come up," she said when we were on the porch. "Smell?" I couldn't help but smell. The smoke wasn't thick, but the burnt smell was strong. It was getting cool again. It cools off fast on nights like tonight, when there's no cloud cover. The smoke must have been pretty thick higher up though, because I couldn't really make out the sky. I sat down on the top step. "Should we do something?"

Jaydie just went back to her pacing. I knew she was worried so I asked her again. "Is there something you think we should do?"

"I don't know," she said, vaguely annoyed, parting two rags of the plastic for a better look. Whatever she saw, she didn't report it.

After a while the smoke seemed to be getting thicker, and I was getting cold, so I went in. At least I thought — but chose not to say — we don't have to worry about the house burning. I was sure it was too far across the bay for live sparks to fly. I sat near the stove and tried not to think.

Jaydie had to come in. The air inside was starting to smell of fire. Seeping in through all the leaky places we hadn't patched. "It's really thick," she said.

"Well?" I figured she'd be ready to answer now.

"I think we'd better go down by the beach. On the Gulf side. If we keep low the smoke should blow over us."

"It's chilly out there," I said quietly. "Spend the night?" Most of her plans have been pretty good, though. She thought of keeping the wheelbarrow upriver, for instance, and when all those people died Jaydie was the one who pulled the few still-functional souls together to dig the mass grave by the Baptist church. She was raised a Unitarian, so I thought that choice of location a nice touch. Right pantheistic of her. Of course, it was the only churchyard in town. Anyhow, I don't argue any more unless her schemes seem outrageous.

"Who knows?" she said. "Let's take some blankets and we'll see." She went to wake Miss Audrey, talking directly into her ear.

"Juli, will you carry Sylvia?" I knew Jaydie was going to ask me that. "She's too heavy for me. It'll just be easier if we get down there without waking her up." Sylvia's real skinny, but she is nine.

It took us a long time to get down to the beach. On the way Miss Audrey started her whimpering routine. The smoke made our eyes water and it hurt to breathe. I had wrapped the kid completely in a blanket, more to keep the smoke out than the cold.

We got down to the beach and nestled ourselves into the lee of Macnamara's sea wall. Jaydie was right. The air smelled of burn, but it wasn't very smokey down there. Miss Audrey whimpered for a while until she drifted off. "I'm cold," she kept saying. I felt like jamming a sock into her mouth. She and Sylvia curled up together in the blankets we had brought. Jaydie walked up and down on the beach for a while, and then she took off her clothes and went in the water. I couldn't see her too well but I heard the splash of her kicking now and then.

2

Some days the stillness makes me dizzy. I am lying naked on my back on the sand, staring into the empty sky. The air is mild, the sun is hot. The bleached wooden planks of Macnamara's balcony cantilever out above the beach; its edge cuts the top off my field of vision. There is nothing else up there but blue.

The fire was two or three days ago. We haven't gone across to look. With the load of wood I brought back that day, and this warm turn in the weather, we haven't had to. I guess we're afraid to survey the damage. The attack of the reptiles never materialized, but I don't like to imagine what is left of the woods. It's still smoking a little. We smell the char when the wind is right.

These empty winter skies were the first thing I came to love after Richard and I moved down here. This luminous clarity that passes the full heat of the sun. Really, I should be more careful. I know so much exposure isn't healthy. Skin cancers and all that. Richard used to cover his face and forearms with a sunscreen lotion every morning. Routinely, all year round. Of course, his skin was much fairer than mine.

I can hear someone walking toward me up the beach,

sand squeaking out from under footsteps. It must be Jaydie. She was gone when the rest of us got up this morning. I fed the other two, as I usually do. Jaydie's not one for cooking. She enjoys goading me into it because I used to do it for a living and she knows I have that cook's disease, always needing to see people eat. "Julian," she says.

I raise myself onto an elbow. "Morning. What you got?" She had set down two pails.

"I've been raking oysters," she says. "Want one?"

"I've never turned down an oyster yet," I tell her. Jaydie opens a couple of big ones. She uses the knife that flaps in its sheath at her hip whenever she has clothes on, tied on with a length of ratty nylon cord. That knife used to be Bullie's, though Jaydie's never said so. Its point has snapped off blunt, so it resembles a chisel, and she uses it as her all-purpose tool. I can tell by her light flicks of the blade against the insides of the shells as she cuts the oysters free that she's in a pretty good mood. "Too bad you didn't bring saltines and Tabasco," I tell her.

"Yeah," she says, with a little one-syllable chuckle. I don't mind the silences that much, but I like it better when she talks.

"So listen," she says. "I think it's about time to harvest prickly pears. I was noticing how ripe they are when I was up on the beach before. They won't be much good if we let the frost get them again. Look." She reaches into one of her pails and brings out a ripe one to show me, holding it up with spread fingers to avoid the tufts of needles on its waxy crimson skin. "Want a taste?"

"Do dogs like bones?"

"I give up. I haven't heard anybody bark lately." She

peels it with her knife, holding it balanced on one end with splayed fingers.

I rest a disc of the fruit on my tongue. It has the texture of watermelon and the tang of raspberries. My mouth puckers so I have to chew and swallow it, seeds and all.

"Was there a lot of fruit up that way?"

"There's some," she says. "But I think the most cactus is out on the islands. On Horseshoe especially. Remember?"

"I do. Want to go today?"

"I need to swim," she says, standing up and shedding her clothes. "But we can go after while."

I'm sitting up cross-legged now, savouring the rest of the sliced prickly pear. Juice dribbles down my chin and into my lap, catching in red droplets on the dark hairs of my thighs. I like the deep leather colour of my skin, but I laugh when I think how once this suntan would have been considered glamorous. There's nothing glamorous now about my body. It's true I'm thin, but in other times this would have been called gaunt. Little empty wrinkles of skin drape over my abdomen where the bones of my hips jut, and when I stand there are wizened pinches of skin where my ass comes down to my thighs. I like my body, though, and the way I move, knees a little bent, gliding, on a low centre of gravity. I didn't always have this balance. I used to be heavier. Not fat, but a lot thicker than I am now. I don't mind the physical changes. The exercise is fine, and we have a pretty good diet. Fresh seafood and occasional small game, and stuff we gather, the beach peas that grow on delicate vines above the tide line in the spring, and in the summer those colourless pulpy wild squashes that in the old days kids used to throw at the seawalls just to see them splat apart. And fruits from the stunted citrus, mango and avocado trees Miss Audrey started from seed a long time ago, which we have to take so much care of in winter because they don't really thrive this far north. It's a light diet, and a pretty healthy one. Sometimes I crave a slice of bread and butter so bad it hurts.

Jaydie's thinner too. Her buttocks look small and pendulous now as she wades out into the muddy sea. Her breasts are that way too. The ribs are visible across her back. We see each other naked all the time. Conventions are more or less observed around Miss Audrey — although I doubt she'd really care — but Jaydie and I seem to have tacitly agreed that a lot of things don't matter any more. Like the agreement not to pry too deeply into each other's thinking, or the one that keeps us celibate. I can't read her mind, but I think we feel pretty much the same overall. Cut adrift and washed up on this bogus paradise shore where things are just easy enough so the true horror doesn't glare through. Each stripped of a lover. Each going through the motions of everyday participation, but encapsulated by disbelief that becomes numbness, and so out of touch. We have watched each other's nakedness a thousand times without either of us expressing desire. I wonder if she thinks because I was lovers with Richard that I'm exclusively gay. The terms are comic and irrelevant, now more than ever. Richard used to answer nosey guests at the inn with an enigmatic lifted eyebrow. "Us?" he would say. "Oh, we're as gay as some, but not as gay as others." Jaydie knows I'm a father, that I was married. But I can't read her mind. I feel the faintest stirring of a hard-on. I lie back down on the sand. Out in the placid

Gulf, Jaydie is kicking water.

A turkey vulture holds his body rigid and traces an effortless circle over me. The fleshy forward parts of his wings make a charcoal stripe. Sun comes through the tips of the feathers making a translucent band behind it. His vulture head is raw-red skin, and he moves it jerkily to angle a better bead on me. Trying to see whether I'm dead probably. What's black and white and red all over? A turkey vulture. Richard blushing. Richard angry.

He did have remarkable colouring, Richard. Very fair skin that could show his feelings right away, and dark eyes under thick dark eyebrows. But his hair was pale grey, barely flecked with its original black, even when I met him, when he was only twenty-six. It was a disarming combination: the fresh, unlined young face topped by that light-shedding, wise man's mane, worn in a loose cut, fluffy on its own without ever being blow-dried.

I met him in the mall at Baton Rouge, the newer one that's like a maze. I was lost of course, trying to find where I'd parked. It was unbelievably hot out, June or July, humidity 300 per cent, and I had spent fifteen wilting minutes searching one section of the parking lot before I gave up and went back inside to cool off. I sat down on a bench across from the entrance to a department store.

I was thinking about my body ageing that day. I was sitting on the bench staring at the creases on the backs of my fingers, permanent creases I realized, deepening into a texture like lizard skin. It could have been the first time I'd really noticed my hands in ten years. I was thirty-five that summer in Baton Rouge.

So I was sitting on the bench staring at my fingers and

past them to the floor. People's feet crossed in front of me. A woman in heels stopped before the display window. Medium-heeled sandals, held to her bare feet by skinny straps. She tilted one foot way back. Probably she did it to release a cramp in her calf, but still it looked like a beckoning motion. She pivoted her foot on the fulcrum of the heel, and took a couple of steps. Her feet were held into the shoes sloppily, and as she shifted her weight her heels would spread off into mid-air. I loved her feet. I made myself not look up. I hadn't been that interested in women lately. Still, if I could have done it without seeing the rest of her, I would have followed those smooth, strapped ankles.

On my next try at finding the car I ran into Richard. I was following a corridor that would lead me outside, but to avoid the heat I dawdled. By the entrance to a men's store I poked through a rack of shirts. Richard was on the raised platform in the centre of the store which served as an office. He caught my attention and nodded hello.

He was wearing a nubby grey silk shirt that hung a little loose across his shoulders — short-sleeved and open-necked, showing the dark hairs on his light forearms and at his throat. He had on dark slacks and black suede espadrilles, without socks. He leaned back, half-perched on the railing of the office platform, as if it were the railing of a cruise liner. The resort look. Maybe he was just doing double duty as a mannequin, trying to push some merchandise. He did have a good head for business.

Later people would always mistake us for brothers. We did have the same shaped faces, with high foreheads and square chins, although his chin had the hint of a cleft in it. And similar builds. But we weren't all that alike in looks. He was a little narrower and taller. I wasn't skinny then, the way I am now. But Richard always had the lean and hungry look.

I guess I am just not done with this thing about Richard, although it had ended long before he went away. Our being lovers, anyway. He made that decision himself for the two of us, which is how he generally preferred things to come down, moving his things into one of the empty guest rooms, sleeping alone after that. I guess I have not forgiven him. How am I going to work this thing about him out of myself when I'm never going to see him again? He might as well have committed suicide, it was that selfish and destructive an act, to leave this safe hammock and slog off across the swamp to whatever Hieronymous Bosch landscape lies up that broken road, where there must be so many fewer resources, and so many more desperate people. And chemical cesspools leaking, and big crazed dogs running in packs — the big ones having long ago eaten the small ones — or so it has been described by the rare passer-by here on Cape Harrier.

Drops fall from my paddle to land in a curve on the surface as I reach for my next stroke. Jaydie is in the stern, paddling soundlessly. A great blue heron flies past a few feet above his own undulating shadow, propelling himself to Horseshoe Island on wingbeats so languid it is a miracle he stays aloft. The bird opens his craw and gives us a slow outraged croak.

"I think Sylvia is doing much better, don't you?" Jaydie

says over the hollow lapping of water on the aluminium hull. "I had a more or less normal conversation with her yesterday, and she — well, she faded in and out a little bit, but it was a definite improvement." Sylvia has been pretty well shut down since Bullie died. He wasn't one of the ones who caught the sickness. He died after that. Sylvia saw it happen. I never have pried the details loose from Jaydie. I suspect Sylvia inherits her tendency to fade in and out from Jaydie.

"What did you talk about?" I'm sure she knows I'm not that interested in Sylvia. What I am interested in is having a more or less normal conversation with Jaydie. It's always a refreshing change. It reminds me how life used to be in the society of competent adults, who kept their nightmares tucked under their pillows.

"I was telling her about schools and learning, about reading. It's hard for her to imagine the whole situation. She was never even in a playgroup. Living down here there were never enough kids of the same age. Reading seems as foreign to her as Chinese. I feel bad about that. I think it's my fault for not introducing her to it."

"I'm sure it wouldn't seem to have anything to do with her world, reading," I say. "I mean, all the things that would have made it familiar to a kid, the mail coming every day, magazines, even the fucking TV guide, she never sees."

"There are books around, though." Jaydie's voice flutters. "We've got books. I — never read anymore myself."

"Yeah, maybe if she saw you reading as a routine thing."

"And of course," Jaydie says, drawing her paddle from

the water crooked so it splashes, "when you read you go down to the inn to do it. So she never sees that either." There is an edge to her voice.

I weigh several responses to this observation of the distance I maintain. When I moved in with them at Miss Audrey's, after Bullie died, after Richard split, when there was no one left but us, it was an arrangement of mutual need. It's grown to something more than that in this year, and specifically with Jaydie. The two of us have developed a trust that is sometimes the only thing I'm sure of. Still, I never said I was giving up my privacy. But I decide not to take this as a challenge. "Yes, my books are at the inn," I say.

"Do you just read them over and over? I mean, haven't you run out of ones you haven't read before?"

"I've gone through all the houses and gathered up the books I thought I'd be interested in. Besides, I read them slowly. Sometimes I just sit with one opened on my lap. Sometimes they remind me too much."

"I guess that's how come I stopped reading. It reminds me too much, too. I tried this book of science fiction stories I came across. That was a little better, otherworldly, so it didn't resemble how things used to be that much. But every few stories there would be a survival story, you know, shipwrecked on a moon of Venus or something. And that reminded me too much of now." She laughs.

"Maybe we're actually on a moon of Venus."

"Hmm. Maybe nothing ever really happened except this stretch of the coast got blasted into orbit somewhere."

"Yeah, somewhere real obscure, like Jupiter or Pluto."

"Oh, definitely it would be someplace obscure," she agrees. "Obscurity has always been Cape Harrier's prime attraction. You know that, you tried to make it here in the tourist trade."

"Hey, is this potential material for a game of What Happened?" That's another of the games Jaydie and I play. When we're in good moods. Too bad we didn't invent it until after Richard went away. He would have dug it. No, on second thoughts, he would have taken it much too seriously. It's a question he really wanted answered. In the game we develop scenarios to explain why things fell apart. Since we are pretty much in the dark about the true reasons, the possibilities are endless. What Happened has two rules. One, we go a sentence at a time, taking turns building up a story. Two, no nuclear wars allowed. For one thing, the decline was much too gradual. How could we possibly locate it at any one explosive moment? I remember people complaining that things were falling apart for my whole adult life. And certainly since Vietnam. But about the only thing we know for sure is that if it had been a nuclear war we wouldn't be here to entertain ourselves with all these speculations.

The low green streak of Horseshoe Island gains resolution as we approach, taking on a profile of palm tops and feathery casuarinas. I used to think Horseshoe got its name from its shape, a nearly closed curve of flat sand beach aimed southwest into the Gulf that encircles a mangrove lagoon. But once I was out here with Richard in the springtime, and we decided that the name had to be because of the horseshoe crabs, fucking in piles of six and fifteen and twenty, burrowing into the sand just below the waterline. Richard yelled out in horrified delight when he saw them. The island never has been inhabited, and to paddle out here, driven over the water by your own sweating body, felt like a true step beyond, into the wilderness. Now everything is wilderness, or going that way. Anyhow Richard, in his role as front man at the inn, was really good at sensing the right combination of a gentle day and guests who were ready to make that crossing. He would start on them cheerily at breakfast and before they knew what had happened he was pushing them off in the canoe, with a picnic basket. "Give me your watches," he would command, palm out. "You won't need them." Invariably they would return to us sunburned and grateful at dusk, never suspecting that this was Richard's way of carving out some private time for himself and me. I've got to hand it to him for that. He never did let things stop him from getting what he wanted.

We've got our paddling rhythm going now, Jaydie and me. She keeps an eye to when I'm tired and have switched sides, and she switches to compensate without losing a stroke, without our discussing it. We're flying over the placid bay, our two paddles dipping and rising neatly together, making no disturbance.

Jaydie steers us toward the mouth of the lagoon. We slow up and drift around the point, sending five hundred brown ducks into an explosion of flight. They vanish like smoke over the trees, leaving the water's surface dented all over like hammered metal. Our prow bumps the sand.

On the Gulf side, a thicket of cactus curves in a swath down the beach, flat green lobes studded with red prickly pears. Jaydie and I carry pails from the canoe.

"Oh, let's get a lot," Jaydie says with the excitement of a child.

"Sure. It looks like Christmas out here, doesn't it, all red and green. It would be about Christmas time now, don't you think, maybe a little after."

Jaydie's face falls, and for a second it looks like she will drop her bucket too. Oh shit. Now I've shut her up again. I was enjoying the talk. I always was a clod around people who get emotional over Christmas and birthdays. "I'm sorry, Jaydie."

She regains her grip on the bucket. "For what?" she asks, chin up, flashing her so-what-if-I-don't-have-a-date-to-the-prom smile. "Hey, let's get to work," she says heartily, turning her back.

So we make our way along the beach picking fruit. It's a windless day, waves of heat radiating off the sand. I'm wearing stiff old leather-palmed work gloves and a pair of ragged long pants. There's a rip in the index finger of my right glove and of course I soon jab my finger with cactus needles. Inside the gloves my palms are sweating.

Jaydie passes me on her way to dump a bucketful into the canoe. We have different picking styles. She moves along the beach rapidly, taking fruit only from the edge of the thicket. Maybe this is to avoid getting scratched. She's wearing just a short piece of cloth wrapped around her hips like a sarong. Or maybe it's her need to keep moving all the time. Or to get away from me. Maybe all this regular chat has made her feel too exposed. Maybe I really upset her with that Christmas jazz. But she smiles as she goes back down the way, and calls encouragement. Me, I've worked my way deep into the bush, surrounded now by blades of cactus that would be so inviting —

succulent and pillowlike — if they weren't so lethal. I must be a fool to get in here like this. It's all I need, to lose my balance and fall. Julian the human pin cushion.

After eight or ten buckets the canoe is pretty well loaded. "We've got so many we'll have to try putting them up again. They'll go bad before we can eat them all, otherwise." Last time we tried to preserve prickly pears they grew an ugly grey fungus.

"Your department," Jaydie says brightly. "I'll peel. Want to swim?"

It's so hot that I don't hesitate. I drop my pants and wade in. Out here facing the open Gulf the water is clear, and the bottom is sand rather than muck, a shallow descending shelf that reaches miles out. The shallowness keeps the surface calm, like a lake. The waves break way out there where it drops off. Or so I have been told. This is as far out as I've ever gone. The water tingles, cool around my calves.

We walk out. When we are thigh deep, Jaydie dives forward and swims away. I sit down on the sandy bottom and play my fingers over its rippled surface. The water comes to my shoulders, cool, pushing at my buoyant self, rocking me gently. I count the shells that litter the bottom, and watch the sun rocking gently, halfway down the afternoon sky, and peer down at the bubbles of air tangled in the hairs of my crotch.

After a while Jaydie swims up somewhere behind me. I can hear her kicking. Now she is touching my shoulders, sliding her hands around my chest. Slowly she floats around to face me, using my torso as a pivot. She's never done this before. Still, I don't feel surprised. She squeezes me hard. "Juli," she breathes.

I hug her back. The water pushes at us lightly, tipping us. I am losing my balance and Jaydie is all over me now, gentle and everywhere, like the sea, tugging me along in small waves. I go with her.

Her hard body. The scratch of sand on my ass. Our lightness in the water. She tastes of salt all over. This is happening so slowly I can barely think. The water is soft and I hear breakers somewhere. She circles around me floating as I sit tipping in the water. She straddles my waist and I am entering her, she is taking me in, unfolding smooth and wet like the water but warm and close. This is happening so slowly I am losing my balance. Surf is rolling over us, or we are stirring the calm surface. A flight of skimmers dip the water all around. A laughing gull cries in my ear.

I come. I am on my back now in shallow water, leaning up on one elbow, and Jaydie is all over me still but collapsed, her forehead on my chest, her chin dipping the water. The water laps and tugs at us. I'm still inside her.

I came. Did she? I wasn't paying attention. I've sometimes had trouble telling, with a woman. That's one thing simpler with a man. The physical responses aren't such mysteries. Like with Marian, my ex-wife, whole years could go by between times when — oh, shut up head. Jesus, Julian. You've still got your dick inside her. Just be here. Just be here. Now I feel cold, half out of the water like this.

We start back in silence. The sun is low. A gleaming path leads to it over the bay. The silence worries me, and this thing we have done that could change everything, that must change something. I almost wish we hadn't. But it was nice. I want to hold her. Right now. As soon as we get back. I want to stop being alone. But this woman is nuts. And I need to guard my space. I wish she'd say something. "Jaydie?"

"Hm?"

"Are you OK?"

"Um hm. Are you?"

"Um hm."

"Good."

I open my mouth to ask something else, but then I shut it and am glad she's behind me so she couldn't have noticed. I was going to ask her why she did it — why now, what had changed to make her want to. But then I remembered that I was part of it too.

3

Dawn. There's a slow dripping outside. Not a hard rain, and no wind in the palms, either. If this were my bed I could look right out the window. But Jaydie has hers placed so you have to twist around. It's a drizzle maybe. But it doesn't usually drizzle around here. Either it's dry, or there'll be quick afternoon thunderstorms, raining to beat the band.

A lot of unfamiliar sensations waking up here in Jaydie's room. The pale light sifting in from behind us. Jaydie's body, flung across the bed, touching me at the shoulder, at the thigh. Our first morning together. Will there be more? We haven't talked about it.

When we got back from Horseshoe last night, Miss Audrey and the kid were sitting on the porch floor in the dusk, their two pairs of legs spread out to form a diamond around a pile of pecans they were cracking. We could hear their singing as we climbed the path to the house. It's a song Miss Audrey croons now and then when she is in her more communicative state, her own fractured version of "How High the Moon". She sometimes accompanies it with an elliptical monologue about the days she managed a jazz club in the French Quarter in New Orleans. In other versions of this story she was the featured act in the piano bar at the Pontchartrain Hotel, but in still other tellings she was only the dining room hostess at the Hotel San Carlos in Pensacola. For all I know she did all three, and it wouldn't surprise me if she comes up with some other vaguely connected past lives. Her lyrics to "How High the Moon" don't make any sense, but Sylvia loves to sing it. Sylvia can't carry the tune but she makes up for that with enthusiasm. She is never more animated than when she's singing along with the old woman. They're two of a kind, Sylvia and Miss Audrey.

I was feeling real slow, from the sun and the canoeing, and from the sex and the silence. Jaydie was in front going up the path and I was watching her rag of a sarong flutter around her hips and the flapping of that knife in its sheath.

Miss Audrey left off in the middle of a verse as we approached. "Well, where have you all been?" she asked.

Jaydie didn't answer. Instead she went over and put her hand on the child's head, roughing her hair a little.

"We're eating nuts, Mom," Sylvia said stupidly, tilting her head back and looking up into Jaydie's face.

"We were on the island, getting prickly pears," I explained to Miss Audrey. I always feel compelled to deal with her normally when she is being coherent.

"Julian Heald, I swear you tickle me to death," Miss Audrey said with a bucktoothed grin. "I have lived around here most of my life and you are the first person I ever knew who would eat those things. Pecan?" She held out a gracious handful of nuts. She might have been offering a gin and tonic. A gin and tonic would have been just about right. The liver spots on Miss Audrey's hand seemed to have spread since the last time I looked at them. But maybe it was just the cocktail-hour light, and my doubtful vision that made them seem that way.

"Thanks," I said, taking some pecans.

"Jane?" She offered them to Jaydie. Miss Audrey does not employ nicknames. Jaydie shook her head no, and just stood there with her hand on Sylvia's ruffled hair.

"Now, Julian," Miss Audrey began. "I have been meaning to speak to you about pruning those azaleas. You know it can't wait any longer because those buds will be making, and you certainly don't want to nip the buds." She stopped, a puzzled smile on her face, replaying the lines to reveal the pun.

"Yes, ma'am," I said, not smiling, looking at Jaydie, who was watching the last streaks of pink leave the sky.

"Really," Miss Audrey went on, "it would be proper to fertilize and water them now, too. Oh, for a bag of 8-8-8!" I gave her a sharp look. It's a rule that we don't sit around longing for things we can't have. Like bags of fertilizer. Out loud, anyhow. Dotty as she is, Miss Audrey knows that. "I don't suppose we could use some of the compost on them?" she asked hopelessly.

"No, Ma'am," I said. "You know we need that for the fruit trees and the garden. And water is pretty short right now, too."

"Yes, of course. Well. Wasn't it a lovely day today! So warm."

"Yes, it was."

"Unseasonal, don't you think? What month would you say it is, Julian?"

"I wouldn't have any idea," I muttered, looking at

Jaydie, who still had her hand on the kid's head. Miss Audrey retains the infuriating ability to carry on this kind of endless chatter about the weather and the weddings of lost relations and the funerals of forgotten jazz players. It's how she was raised, I guess. But I don't know where she gets the energy for it, unless she stores it up in her dormant periods. Audrey Eloise Euless. I guess they called her Audrey Eloise as a child, running it together into one word. I can just hear it, her mother — or a black cook, more likely — standing on this stoop at the top of the hill yelling "Audreyeloise!" into the four directions, "Audreyeloise, supper!" No one calls like that any more. We've lost our tongues.

Miss Audrey kept it up until I felt like belting her. It didn't help any that Jaydie was being so quiet. All she said were a few words as she helped Miss Audrey to the outhouse and then put her and Sylvia to bed. It was still nice and warm, and I stayed on the porch. "Sing to me, mom," I heard Sylvia whine, and Jaydie sat with them in the kitchen for a while singing a lullaby, "Sweetest Little Baby." I think nine is a bit old to have your mother singing you lullabies, but I try to keep my nose out of Jaydie's child-rearing. I wasn't so hot at that myself. Besides, in my opinion she really sings it for Miss Audrey.

Jaydie stepped out onto the porch for a minute, but she didn't say anything and then she turned and I could hear her going to her own room and shutting the door. Any other day Jaydie's silence wouldn't have bothered me much, but after the afternoon on the island it just didn't seem right.

I walked down the hall and pushed open the door of her

room. I could see she was lying on the bed but I couldn't tell if she was looking at me. "Can I sleep with you?"

"Well," she said. "I thought you'd never ask." Jesus Christ, how are you supposed to act with somebody like this? Maybe she thinks she's speaking sometimes when she's only thinking. Maybe she is that far gone. I took off my jeans and got into bed with her. It was awkward, but it was interesting too. It took us a long time to find a comfortable way to lie together, partly because the room was still so warm. We didn't make love then, but I don't think either of us slept much. Every time I shut my eyes I would see shifting images of cactus pads and prickly pears, of the sun-spangled Gulf tilting away. When we did do it, later in the night, it was long and slow and deliberate.

She's still asleep now, but I have to pee. I extract myself from the bed as gently as I can. Jaydie sleeps on. Outside now, I understand the dripping sound. It is fog, heavy and opaque, condensing at the points of each palm frond into drops that patter against the tin roof and go splat on the stones of the garden path. Fog is odd at this time of year, but then it has been so warm, and with the water in the Gulf so cool — or maybe it's later in the year than I think. Probably there are survivors in other places, persons of more meticulous temperament than any of us here, who keep calendars with notches on tree stumps or with pencil stubs on the inside covers of books, or by counting phases of the moon, people who would know without hesitation whether it's been three years now or four, and who could tell us whether it's January or March, so I would know if this fog is a freak or just the natural turning of the winter into spring. Unless the weather cycles themselves have gone haywire. But I don't know about that. There has to be something that remains steady. Doesn't there?

Pissing, I notice little flakes of dried come on the tip of my dick. I'll rinse them off, but later. This sex could be habit forming. Or it might be the physical intimacy I like, more than the actual sex. Sex can get so complicated. I mean, for instance, Jaydie could get pregnant. Now there's something I haven't had to worry about for a long time. There is something we will definitely have to discuss.

I'm sitting on a stool in the kitchen doorway, getting ready to smoke some of Richard's pot. Of course, he wasn't here to plant or harvest this last crop. But, of the two of us, he was the genuine pothead, and the one who first saved seed to plant. When he left he took the stash, and the pipe. He claimed he would need it to barter with. I thought he just wanted it for himself, but I didn't care enough to argue about it. Later I discovered he had left the Band-Aid tin full of seeds. I passed a lot of time last summer whittling a pipe while the plants were maturing.

Shots, across the water. That'll be Everest, out on Horseshoe, hunting ducks or something. Everest grew up on these islands, and he still lives in a mobile home out in the swamp with his wife and kids. There used to be a rutted track you could get to it on, though you needed a four-wheelie in the rainy season, but I imagine that's pretty well grown over. When we go now, we go by boat as far as we can, and then in from the salt-marsh on foot. Everest probably thinks a foggy morning like this is a good time to go duck hunting. He would be able to find the lagoon on Horseshoe blindfolded. According to Miss Audrey, the Thibault family was one of the first to settle around the cape — stray Cajuns is my hunch — but by the time it got down to Everest's generation they were pronouncing Thibault "Tie-balled", and had lost any clear recollection of their origins. The year I was supplementing our income by taking the U.S. Census in this end of the county, theirs was one of the households I had to visit. That was when I met Jenny, Everest's wife. When I asked her the question about the family's ethnic background she stared at me like I was talking Arabic. "Where are your people from?" I probed. "Here," she said simply. "Well, I mean before that," I said. "We just come from here. Well, my grandmomma come from Alabama somewhere. I been to Orlando one time myself, to Disney World." I filled in the blank on the census form with "N/A". I liked her though. She had planted big confused patches of vegetables and flowers all around the dull aluminium trailer house. She had long stringy black hair and a ready smile that showed bad teeth. She offered me a can of Bud and wanted to rap. It seemed she already knew who I was and she must have been curious. I couldn't blame her. We were the only faggots in town. I liked the bluntness of that curiosity. Jenny wore a pair of glasses held together at the hinge with a safety pin. Later, bounding back to the state road in Richard's pickup, that struck me. It was one of those safety pins with a pastel blue plastic catch, made for use with diapers. "Three children," she had answered. Ages six, nine and eleven. They'd all have been out of diapers for years. And anyway, wouldn't Jenny have used disposables?

Everest used to hang out with Bullie some. They used to hunt together. Bullie was into guns, but Jaydie and I aren't, so after he died we decided to lay his guns and the rest of his ammo, and some boxes of shot-gun shells we had come across in other houses, on Everest. Everest still hunts, and we barter for some of what he gets. He had a twin brother who got killed when they were both in Vietnam. The word is that he came home with a drug habit. I suppose he had trouble laying his hands on junk down here. But he tells stories of serving as navigator for various smuggling operations along this coast, and about the high quality coke he used to get as his pay. He used to drink a fair quantity of beer, too, and had a respectable gut developing, but now that there's no more Bud and fried pork rinds to snack on he's become thinner, like the rest of us. He's about my age, mid-forties, and his curly blond hair has thinned out to a bald pate. Now there are wine-coloured splotches on his scalp, and on his shoulders. Too much sun, I guess. I didn't trust Everest much at first, but probably I was just scared of him, him being a cracker. He turns out to be pretty solid, and a hell of a nice guy, too. None of the Thibaults got sick when all those other people did — the grandfather was still alive and with them then, too, as I recall — and Jaydie and I once theorized that the sickness could have had something to do with the town water supply, since those guy's have got their own well. But then, it was such a surface thing, like an invisible cloud of something acid had settled onto people's skins. I just don't know.

I lift the top off the clear plastic work bowl of the food processor. That's where I stash the smoke now. Richard would get a kick out of that. He gave it to me for my birthday one year. Honestly, I couldn't help resenting that a little bit. In the division of things at the inn I ran the kitchen, and so it felt like being given a dishrag, or an eggbeater. Is that ridiculous? Of course the food processor had possibilities beyond the purely utilitarian. We were getting quite a reputation on the foodie grapevine in this part of the country. For a couple of years there they were coming from Atlanta and New Orleans, the BMWs parked in the weed patch next to Richard's little pickup, after one of my recipes was run in the request column in *Gourmet* and the inn was mentioned in a piece on out-of-the-way destinations in the travel section of the Sunday *Constitution*. The processor, of course, is useless now, like most of the things in this kitchen, but I've left it right where it sat. This was my domain then, and it's my private space still. I scoop a bowlful of pot and put the lid back on the work bowl.

Two more shots. If that's Everest hunting ducks, I guess we'll be seeing him later on. Roast duck will be a nice change. Maybe I'll mash up some kumquats and boil them down into a sauce. I'll pack Everest up a jar of smoke to trade. He's probably running low. Poor Everest. He always complains about making do with this home-grown. He was spoiled on Thai sticks and all that uncut cocaine. Well, we've all come down a peg or two. Wait till he finally runs out of ammunition and we have to learn to get by without fowl and meat too. No, if it takes his bare hands, Everest will figure out how to trap game.

It's still foggy out on the Gulf, but over the land it has burned away some. The filtered sun shines weakly off the hood and roof of Richard's Datsun truck which tilts on dead tires in the yard here below me. It used to be bright yellow with an orange stripe down each side but it's been bleached almost white, and the stripe has gone pink, along with the logo above it, "Li'l Hustler". When I once asked him if he'd bought that particular model because of its name, he denied it. But that's exactly the kind of thing he would have done. Besides, Richard didn't always tell the truth.

Smoke rises in a blue plume from the bowl of the pipe. I am torn between covering the bowl after each hit to smother out the coal and burn less pot, and letting it burn to prolong the life of the butane lighter. Today I just let it go. The pot is a renewable resource. There'll be more next summer, after this batch runs out. The butane is finite and dwindling. Then again, what the hell. We already take care to keep a small fire going all the time, even in the worst heat of the summer. Some relic or other from how things were gets used up every now and then. I kind of like that. It makes me feel less weighed down.

Well, what if Jaydie should get pregnant?

I'm having trouble making myself focus on that, and I'm not sure why. Because it would tie me to her? But I already am. And I have no intention of leaving here. Because something might go wrong, medically? We're on our own that way anyhow. Any one of us could drop dead tomorrow or contract some lingering fatal disease, or some rapid fatal disease. Or drown or get chomped by an alligator. We just can't walk around worrying all the time. So what's my problem? I remember so many people of our generation saying it was too dangerous and uncertain a world to bring children into — but those circumstances have gone by. We still live with uncertainty, but there is peace here, survival of a sort. It wouldn't be that bad a place to grow up.

Look at Jenny and Everest's kids. Growing up in the wild — a much more wholesome childhood than even they would have had before. No TV to dull their senses or shoddy rural state school education to limit the possibilities, to cap their ambitions. For a while Everest used to row them over here every other morning and I would spend a couple hours trying to work on reading with them. Sylvia would sit with us, too. But there was no point to it other than immediate diversion, and while the Thibault kids were alert, and gabby enough, there sat Sylvia, dumb as a stump. We gave that up pretty quick, Everest and me, in an impromptu parent-teacher conference on the swaying dock one afternoon.

"Seems like the kids just come for the boat ride," Everest told me. "I think they're wasting your time, Juli."

"I think Emory is learning a lot," I answered half-heartedly. "And you know, I've got time to burn."

"Not really," he said, "taking care of Miss Audrey and the girls like you have to." He was standing up in his skiff, leaning his elbows on the planks of the dock, looking up at me. I traced the network of blood vessels on his balding forehead.

"How about wearing a hat more often, Everest?"

"Shit," he said. "I think it's just as well to give up this school thing, Julian. Unless you really don't want to."

"Hey. It's not that important to me." I didn't want him to think I was insistently intellectual or anything. He grinned agreement and the web of capillaries on his cheeks crinkled up. His arms looked bad too. "I really think you should wear a hat, Everest. And long sleeves." He ignored me. I was glad the school thing got settled like that, though. I had regretted the project from the minute Jaydie and Jenny had talked me into it. Spending time with kids generally gives me the creeps, and every time I really considered my haphazard curriculum — and what the carcass of Western knowledge might look like in a generation or two, it just made me want to lie down in the sun and go to sleep. Which I do too much as it is.

I guess this whole transition down from civilization hasn't been all that smooth. When I think back on these recent years, it's easier to leave out the sticky parts, the uncontrollable things that happened, pictures of the people who couldn't cope, people who couldn't help spilling over their edges like the spastic crayon marks in a small child's colouring book. Oh, I didn't have any trouble myself. I guess I always had expected the world to come apart. If it wasn't at the very top of my mind when I talked Richard into moving down here, getting to someplace where we could avoid the heaviest weight of the collapse was my unconscious motive. So I wasn't surprised. What I felt was more like relief. Not that strong a feeling, either.

But a lot of people didn't have such an easy time as I had. Bullie, for instance. He could be a nice enough guy. Real affable, the perfect bartending personality. You could rap at him all day long, end up feeling he was your best friend, and not realize he hadn't said a thing. He was wiry and tall, with short sandy hair that receded at either temple, good-looking in a wolfish sort of way — strong teeth, a sharp chin. He had this frustration, though, this anger that could boil up in him like some accidental mix of chemicals in a laboratory beaker. Which was strange because before when he would get violent it really was a chemical reaction, from drink. But later on, when there wasn't any liquor, he was still randomly explosive. It was when he started beating Jaydie up that she took herself and the kid and moved up the hill with Miss Audrey. She still used to hang out with him after that, but I guess the move let her do it more on her own terms. I don't know what finally happened there, except that she and the kid were with Bullie the day he died, and Jaydie dug a grave and buried him by herself, before she even told anyone else it had happened. Miss Audrey, who was a lot clearer then, said she thought that had been real brave of Jaydie, letting the rest of us avoid seeing one more corpse. I often wonder.

For Richard and me, it was still going OK as things began to fall apart. What outside pressures there had once been, the chores of keeping the inn going dropped away. We would stay in bed in the mornings, reading or making love, and when we were no longer making love, just watching the birds pass and the light shift on the surface of the Gulf. I can see him lying there now, on his stomach, the smooth skin of his thighs and back gleaming. I felt as if we had been granted a deepest wish, for quiet and seclusion, and time — the same vision I had in mind when we left the city in the first place, but one we could never sustain while we had to make beds and dinners, make a living. He didn't feel the same, it turned out. But it was something I had so longed for that I seduced myself into thinking it could last. The relationship, I mean. In the beginning, I didn't bother with what was going on, or not going on, around us. I just let myself fill with the lapping sea and its saltiness, the salt tastes of Richard's body and the rhythm of his breathing. And at first he seemed to do the same. We kept pretty much apart from everyone else in town, ignored the worrisome signals from the outside world, did not join in the speculation. I guess that I would have eventually broken that bubble. But it was Richard, in his relentlessness, who did it first.

The door of his old truck is wide open below me. The truck rusting in the position he left it that last frantic time he tried to pick up something on the radio. It was remarkable how long the battery held enough juice to power that radio, months and months and months. The first times, Richard did it on the sly, like he was sneaking a cigarette behind the boys' gym. When I came around the side of the house one time to see him sitting in the pickup hunched intently over the dial, I felt a little sting of betrayal. The air going out, leaving me limp. "What are you doing?" I asked him, leaning in through the passenger window. He was sitting in the truck like he was ready to gun it and zoom off. Richard looked at me for a minute, long enough to sort through and discard a variety of stories. Of course there was only one that fit. "Don't you want to know, Juli?" he asked finally in a dead voice. "Don't you need to be sure? Don't you sometimes think it might have been just us, here, this forgotten little bump on the coast, and everything back to normal everywhere else?" His face looked dark — not angry, lifeless. That was partly the beard, thick on his cheeks and shadowing his mouth. That was another of Richard's betrayals, the beard thing. When we first moved down here we decided together to give up shaving. Why bother to scrape your face in a town where half the adults don't bother to wear shoes? But sure enough, it wasn't long before I walked in on him lathered up, razoring it off. After that he would change his facial hair-do every so often, now a moustache, now a Van Dyke, now his pearly skin shaved clean. After the end, he didn't have any choice but to let it grow. But now and then I think he finally took off out of here because he craved to find a razor blade, and thought he might somewhere back up that road — so that he could clean up, and splash with bay rum, and run a comb through his silky white hair. He sat there fiddling with the radio dials. "What have you picked up?" I asked him, hearing the disgust in my own voice.

"Static," he shrugged, still tuning. "I heard something, someone talking, but it faded out and I couldn't catch it. But someone's broadcasting. It means everything's not totally . . . gone."

"We knew that already," I told him. But his ears were glued to the dashboard.

It wasn't even the first time he'd done it, just the first time I caught him. After that he did it all the time. He not only did it, but he made me get involved. When he knew I wasn't interested. Like the big debate about whether the battery would run down, whether we shouldn't start the engine before that happened — there was a bit of gas left in the tank — and let it charge up. About how long it would need to run before it was recharged. Whether it would be more gas-efficient to idle it or to race it. And so on, and so on. And when the battery did finally start to fade, he prowled around among the other cars in town, making me help him carry their batteries back here and jump them together. So that finally we had a mechanic's nightmare patchwork of batteries and cables hooked up, all to fuel this rinky-dink radio in the dashboard of this

Datsun truck, all to fuel Richard's obsession with finding an answer that I don't believe exists. The batteries were all still there when he left, until I tripped over the cables one day and got furious and yanked the whole mess apart. Spilled acid on my leg doing it, too, like a jerk.

But for what? The only signal he ever got clearly enough to understand was of some Christian freaks near Appalachicola. I mean you could recognize the words they were using, but they shot them out in such a jet of panic that you could never gather their meaning. Their broadcast was erratic, you never seemed to hear the same person twice, and each new voice was that much less coherent. Nothing that ever shed any light on the question. Other than that static, and very occasional sounds that might have been squashed voices but were too indistinct to catch. Or maybe they were speaking in Spanish. In the old days, at night, you could pick up Spanish-language stations out here. Beaming across the Gulf from Mexico I guess, or from Texas, or from Tampa for all I ever knew, since I don't understand it and never tried to find out. Spanish-language static, and streams of Baptist fear that eventually dried up into dead air.

I overtake Jaydie on the beach. "Hey," she says, slipping an arm around my waist as we fall into step. "I've been thinking about you."

"Surprise."

"How do you feel?"

"Fine. Like I'm standing at the bottom of a stairway and don't know where it goes. But getting ready to go up."

She laughs. "I like how timid you are, Juli."

"What do you mean," I say, feeling maligned.

"Oh, you know. The way you just sit there behind the face of the Buddha until you've sorted it all out and decided what you're going to do. Once you decide you can be a real tiger."

Now I feel embarrassed. "Well, you don't give much advance warning either."

"Maybe you need new glasses."

"Hey, that's not fair. Of course I need new glasses."

"Oh god." She slips her hand down inside my pants and over my butt as we walk. "Don't take everything so seriously." For Jaydie, this behaviour is downright giddy. I'm usually the cheery one. It's all very disarming. Maybe I'm just stoned. We walk along the water's edge in the dreamy fog. "I brought some pot with me. Want to smoke?" She almost never does.

"Sure." She leads the way to a hollow in the low dune. We smoke a bowl, nestled together in the sea oats, and start making out.

"Hey, don't you think all this contending with the elements is a little, um, juvenile? We could go do it in a bed. With sheets even."

"No. I don't want to get into that, beds and sheets, sleeping in the same room together every night. It's so normal. I want to do it in weird places. Out here under the eye of God. In the back seats of cars."

"Shit."

"Yeah," she sits up excited. "Let's go do it in the back seat of somebody's car. That would be really fun."

"You're out of your mind."

"Possibly. Come on. Get up." She tugs me to my feet.

"Jaydie," I say as we re-enter the town. "What about birth control?"

"What about it? What about defrosting the refrigerator? What's on the tube tonight?"

"Come on, be serious for a second."

"Well, we could use the rhythm method, except we don't have a calendar. Or we could use the withdrawal method. I'll let you decide that one. Or we could just not think about it and see what happens. Here, here's one. Macnamara's Buick wagon. That's perfect. We'll fold down the back seat. If only there were some way to let him know. That fool always used to have his hands all over me. I had to stop Bullie from going after him more than once, when he was drunk. Just perfect. Besides, if I judged those sons of Macnamara right, this old Buick has been pretty well seasoned. Let's see if we can find their come stains."

Jaydie trots over to the old whale of a car. The tail gate won't open, so she goes around to a back door. She has to use the heel of her hand to pound in the button on its rusting handle. The door swings open with a creak, revealing a colony of palmetto bugs, their hard oversize cockroach bodies clicking against one another as they make their leisurely way to the safe dark crack under the seat. The inside of the car releases a steamy mildew, and even though Jaydie proceeds undaunted to fold down the back of the seat, I know there's no chance I'll be able to get it up, in there.

But something else grabs our attention, at first barely perceptible on the breeze: Sylvia's high voice calling in a two syllable plaint. "Mo-om, Mo-om." Jaydie catches it, stays still to listen one time, and takes off running, towards the hill and her child.

4

Sylvia has Jaydie by the hand, dragging her around to the back of the house. "Who is it, Mom?" she bleats. "Who is it?"

Through the thin scrim of fog that lingers above the cape we watch the stranger approach: a slow-moving figure, swathed from head to foot in some colourless fabric, and so obscured. "Who is it?" Sylvia insists. "I can't tell yet, honey," Jaydie says, trying to soothe her.

He is wading across the new pass, shin deep in brown water, holding up his swaddling robes to keep them dry. "Kind of looks like a Hare Krishna," I say. "With the saffron colour bleached out of his sheets by the sun."

"Don't be funny about religious freaks," Jaydie says between her teeth. Sylvia is fairly twitching, and no wonder. The last intruders to appear up this road were a family from Anniston, Alabama, who managed through a tortured round of "who do you know" to find some distant relative of Miss Audrey's whom they claimed as a friend or neighbour. Miss Audrey then felt obliged to invite them to stay in the big house, and for a day or two it seemed like it might work out. This was before Richard split, when he and I were still living at the inn, while Jaydie had her hands full up at the big house with

Miss Audrey and Sylvia. So the additional people might have been a help. But they turned out to be crazed fundamentalists who said they had walked to the coast in the living company of Jesus — he in robes and sandals and an aura as focused as a halogen headlight that enabled them to force-march through the night. The patriarch of the family turned every meal into a tongue-lashing about how the wicked had certainly gotten their deserts now, slapping his kids for emphasis, and Sylvia too, if they got antsy. Then Jaydie found his kids binding Sylvia to the trunk of the live oak with kudzu vines, because she wouldn't answer their questions. Apparently their view of things did not allow for those who had been shocked into silence. Jaydie and I plotted the eviction while Richard rowed out after Everest and Jenny. The old goat was tenacious, but Everest's shotgun seemed to put the fear of God into him all over again. It was Jenny who really came through though. "You people just can't barge in here and take things over," she said, shaking with anger. "And Miss Audrey not well like she is. Go on now, you collect your things and get on out of here." Her three kids stood behind her, erect and supportive as stays in a fence, until she sent them to oversee the children's packing.

"They're harmless, Hare Krishnas," I say now, trying to keep things light. The person is coming slowly closer, mounting the bank of the cut, his body quite erect as he climbs. "Well, those finger cymbals can get annoying, ding, ding, ding." I make pinching motions in the air like finger cymbals dinging. "But they used to put on public feasts, you ever go to one? Oh, it was boring food, Indian food but bland, without any curry, bland split peas, gluey rice. But you've got to admit, any of that would at least be a change."

"Shut up, Juli. You always talk too much when you get nervous," is Jaydie's response.

I am about to protest when Sylvia, who is standing between us, slips her free hand into mine — an expression of confidence, or a choice of the known evil as the lesser, maybe. "Look," she whispers. "There's another one." A second person has appeared where the road emerges from the woods, on the far side of the pass. Small in the distance, he limps toward us. Tension runs between the three of us on the conduit of Sylvia's rigid spindly arms. We stand like a family in a Dorothea Lange photograph — valiant in the face of dust storm and disaster. Only it isn't hard times that stiffens us like this. It's bare mistrust of other people, lack of interest in their condition, the passionate wish that they would leave us alone. Now we will have to suffer more news, new involvements.

The first person has turned around to face his lagging companion. Apparently they are yelling to each other — we can see their gestures. Now the far one points toward us, as if they had not seen us before, and the closer one turns back to face us and waves. He starts toward us again, waving, and the burnous-like garment drops away from his head in the exertion, revealing a falling knot of white hair, a pale beardless face. It is a woman. The other has reached the pass. He does not move with the same balance she has, there is a roll or a limp in his walk, and as he descends the shallow bank he slips and falls to his knees in the water.

The woman turns to go back for him but he waves her on. As fast as she is walking, there is a poise to the set of her shoulders. She is still a way off, adjusting the cloth back over her head, when Jaydie breaks the stony tableau the three of us have been making "We know her, Juli."

"We do?"

"You know them. I don't remember her name. That German woman. They stayed with you and Richard. He's from Brooklyn or New Jersey or someplace like that. If that's him. But I know it's her. I think they bought a place here, too. You know them."

She is calling hello now, and Jaydie is loping down the hill to meet her, with Sylvia right behind. I do know them. Hilde, she's called. Her husband is Bennie Greenspan. Well. It could have been worse. It could have been complete strangers, the unknown, or else someone we're sure we don't want to see. I remember being fond of Hilde and Bennie. Of course there's no telling how it's all changed them.

"How do you do," she is saying to Jaydie as I reach them, shaking hands. I'm not sure Jaydie is going to remember what to do with these manners, she's letting her hand be pumped with a passive half-smile on her face. Sylvia is hiding behind her mother, her fear giving way to shy interest. "This is your little daughter?" Hilde asks, focusing attention like a visiting aunt as the kid shrinks further away. "My, she was just a baby." Sylvia is spared by my arrival. "Ah, Mr Heald," Hilde says. "We were so hoping you would be all right. So nice to see you again."

"Julian," I say, "please."

"Yes," she smiles, with puffy lips. The cloth has dropped from her head again. She is pale-skinned, with a spatter of freckles across her cheeks and nose, and long white hair that has been braided and knotted up onto her head but is falling down anyway in wisps and loops. She draws a big satisfied breath, looking around like any tourist just arrived, taking it all in deep. The rich salt smell. The clean emptiness. "So lovely here, it always was. We have been trying to get back for so long. And your friend? Mr Keller?"

She is terribly thin. Up close, I can see the hollows in her face as she speaks. The shapeless robe she wears conceals it on the rest of her. "Richard's gone," I say. "You must be hungry. Come on."

"Eh," she tries to shrug away the suggestion of ordeal. "Well, it has been a rather difficult journey. And Bennie isn't so well lately. I wasn't convinced we should even try, but he insisted that this was where he wanted to be." She is looking around again, trying to assess what might have changed. "It seems awfully quiet," she observes, hopefully.

"Awfully," Jaydie says. "Julian, go help Bennie, why don't you. Sylvia, you go tell Miss Audrey we have company. But be sure you tell her it's people we know. Friends. Go on."

Hilde goes to the house with Jaydie, but Bennie won't let us feed him yet. He has to have a look at his own place. "We've been on the road for two years," he says. "What do you think? That I could eat first?"

He leads me to the cottage, one of the ordinary small clapboard ones. I guess they didn't have much money, when they bought. It's in the centre of town and, blocked by the buildings along the waterfront, has neither a clear view of sunrise on the bay, nor the sunset and wind off the Gulf. But it would have been a pleasant enough retirement nest, compact and modest, and once it must have had a lovely garden. Now there are rose bushes that range out of control, long attenuated stems straggling in the breeze, a thicket of azalea as high as the eaves. We have to rip a mat of kudzu from the screen door to get onto the porch.

Bennie limps across to the door, and digs into a pocket in his pants. The jingle is like a sudden phrase spoken in the wrong language. Coins? For what? No, he draws out a ring of keys. It is midday, but the overgrowth makes it dark on the porch, and I can only see Bennie's tangled black hair and beard, not his expression. He sorts formally through the keys on the ring and finds one to try, but the door swings open as he puts it into the lock.

"What the devil! Somebody's been in here," Bennie says.

"It was us, Bennie. A few years ago. When it was clear that things had changed. Those of us who were left here went through all the empty houses. Just to see what we had to work with. I don't think we took very much from here. We... I hope you don't mind." As if we had expected Hilde and Bennie, or anybody else, to show up again some day, any more than the Macnamaras, who had chanced, thank God, to be at home, not here, because the end came in the off-season or maybe it was the middle of a work week. Any more than we held our breath now for the reappearance of those whose rotting corpses we had pushed into that big grave. Strange to begin talking about the end with someone who was somewhere else. Will we call things by the same names?

"So my stock is still here?" He is leading the way to the back bedroom, a room that had fascinated us briefly during our ransacking operation. It is stacked high with cartons of strangely useless objects, priced and labeled: Coca-Cola trays, an apparently complete set of *Life* magazines from the forties, each in a plastic bag, little empty bottles in novelty shapes — a racing car, an Indian head — that had once held Avon cosmetics. Bennie begins at once to paw through the boxes, which we had left in a mess. "Help me lift this down," he orders. "Can't you clear that window so I can have some light?" I remember Richard and Bullie and Jenny and me going through these piles, all of us giddy with much-needed comic relief as we unearthed Bennie's flea market merchandise. All except Jenny, really, who somehow didn't get the joke. Probably she could see the use in some of it, the partial sets of pink and green depression glass dishware, the stainless steel flatware with red and yellow celluloid handles. Seeing the prices, she made little gasping noises.

Bennie slows down his inspection after a while. "I guess it's all here," he admits. "I knew it would still be here. One of the reasons I wanted to come back. I had a garage full at my brother's place in Levittown, New Jersey. When we got there? Nothing. Everything torn, broken, ripped off. And I had a mini-warehouse outside Baltimore. I had been putting stuff aside there for years, you know. But that whole side of the city burned to the ground. I always knew a collapse would come, and whoever had saved the things people were going to want would make a killing." He speaks in a tone of instruction and certainty. Now I remember that he and Hilde first came here to spend a few days between weekends at a flea market where they were dealing. Richard had remarked on the cleverness of their arrangement, collecting a pension from some earlier career while travelling the south every winter in a van and trailer on a self-supporting gypsy tour. Richard coaxed him into opening the van and pulling out some of their goods. I think that was the year Bennie paid for their stay with some clunky art deco pottery and the Turner print of flamingos in the blue mirrored frame. "Everybody loves a trade," Bennie had said with a smug look. "Everybody makes out." "These things go for big bucks in Miami or New Orleans," Richard informed me later. To me they just looked tacky; Richard always knew what was hot. Hilde is absent from these horse-trading episodes, in my recollection.

Now Bennie is ready to go, without inspecting the rest of his house. "Yeah," he grins, "I knew at least this much would survive. I knew I should keep it in more than one place. It's convenient anyhow. We're always up and down the east coast, you know, This way we can leave anything we don't want to have with us right now."

"You still have stuff stored in other places?"

This stops him. "Well, not now, I told you what they done to my stuff in New Jersey. You can't carry much now anyway, you know. And people just want real useful items. I hid a pack by the road back there, this morning. Hilde says why don't I, and then I can come back for it, smart girl. We didn't know what things will be like here. Some places we got to and the people there ripped us off right away, what we were carrying. I knew things would be OK here, but Hilde thought — you know, she worries."

"What do you have in your pack, up the road?" I am picturing more of this junk — old postcards, costume jewellery. He's talking as if the trade in collectibles is still happening, business as usual, only on foot.

"Band-Aids, soap. Things like that."

"Jesus. Where did you get that stuff?"

"Ah, ah," he says, turning up his nose. "That's the first question you never ask a dealer. The second one is what I paid. So how's business at your hotel?"

I look at him, trying to figure out if he's serious. Can a question like that still apply, anywhere? But I can't make out his face, he's busy yanking vines away from the screens of the porch, a perfunctory homeowner. "Ready to go?" he asks, not waiting for an answer to his first question. Bennie limps along up the path. He didn't have a limp before, as I remember. But maybe it's the two torn running shoes he wears, which aren't a pair. And he is wheezing when we gain the crest of the hill.

Hilde and Miss Audrey sit side by side on the porch swing. Jaydie squats before them, barefoot on the weathered floorboards. She is telling Hilde, "Yeah, some left, but most died before that. A poison cloud or something. Some people got it and their skin rotted. And some people just didn't. But it scared the ones who didn't, and they left. Most of them went in one big group, like a parade. They all gathered at the gas station, with bundles on their backs, stuffing in more wherever they could, waiting for the late ones. But God, were they crazy to leave! Jumping around, jittering. Dancing around like kids who have to pee. Know what I mean?"

"Some people got it," Hilde repeats, dreamily almost. "And some people just didn't."

"That's how it was," Jaydie says. "You got it, you'd had it."

"Mm," Hilde says. She is rolling a glass of water back

and forth between her two palms like someone in winter drawing warmth off a mug of cocoa. Like somebody thirsty but afraid to drink. "That's how it was with the bumps. A different plague. They got bumps all over their skin, bumps like blueberries, and soft, they would split open and leak. All who got them died. And yet some of us just never got them. Even if you happened to touch the... pus. You just had it or you didn't." She says "plague" like it's the most natural thing in the world. Like "water". Like "morning". Like "mourning".

"Why! Mr Bennie Greenspan!" Miss Audrey says brightly, as we mount the stairs, holding out a limp wrist. As if Bennie is really going to bend and kiss it. Half the time she can't remember her own name, and now she knows his. "How delightful. Julian, why don't you fix Bennie and Hilde a little lunch, sugar." Miss Audrey as hostess. So nauseating.

"You must be hungry," I agree.

"Well," Bennie allows.

I park him in the rocker and go down the porch to the kitchen. When I get back he is uncomfortably asleep, head askew, jaw flapped open. He looks really bad. Jaydie continues, to Hilde: "Bullie — yes, Bill — yes, he died too." She doesn't offer the details.

"I'm so sorry," Hilde replies, leaning forward to put her glass down on the floor and touch Jaydie on the wrist. Jaydie looks up at her, but I'm behind her and can't tell her expression. I'm searching Hilde's forearm for the tattooed numbers. Or no, I remember wrong. It was the rest of her family that died, Jews in the Nazi camps, after Hilde had been smuggled out. Two pictures of herself she once showed me: the first, from before. Before that apocalypse. She's a girl of maybe twelve, plump cheeks and full dark lips, a mass of pale soft hair like a smudge of emulsion on the curving, crinkle-edged photo paper. She's with two older brothers on their verandah, in a suburb of Frankfurt. Behind them, French doors with leaded glass stand open at jarring angles. The other picture is from after. After she hid for two years in the chicken coop of a Dutch family. After the war's end. She is sixteen, or maybe twenty. You can't tell. Much thinner, lips a flat shadow, wearing a dark overcoat and a hat that clings to her skull. Hilde showed me these pictures one time — or maybe I imagined it. Now I am not sure and it seems wrong to ask.

Hilde draws back her hand, her unblemished forearm, but her motion has prompted Miss Audrey, who grabs her by the wrist. "You'll stay the night, of course," Miss Audrey announces. The rest of us look around at one another embarrassed. "Well," Hilde says. "Thank you. We do plan to stay. But you know, we have our house there."

Sylvia who has been perched on the porch railing right behind the swing — as close as she can get right now to Miss Audrey without climbing over Hilde — suddenly jumps off and starts running down the hill. "Everest and them!" she yells. "Everest and them!"

Their rowboat is approaching our dock but I can't make it out well. "Who's all there?" I ask Jaydie.

She stands to look. "The whole family. Hear that, Miss Audrey? Everest and Jenny and their kids are on the way over. You were just wondering about Jenny the other morning."

"Yes," Miss Audrey says. "Yes, I was. Well isn't this just . . . I don't know when we last had such an exciting day."

Hilde, on the other hand, has a panic reaction darting around her face like something trapped. The commotion has wakened Bennie, too. He snorts and wheezes himself upright in the rocker. Hilde goes to calm him down, the effort keeping her own fear in check. Jaydie has seen it, and she leans over the two of them. "It's OK," she murmurs, putting a hand on Hilde's shoulder. "These are good friends of ours."

Everest and Jenny and their kids. They come up the path bearing ducks, and oysters in a bushel basket, and bundles of other stuff. The kids are eleven and fourteen and fifteen now. Named after colleges in their parents' hope that they would make it out of the swamp. Emory and Auburn, the boys, and Sophie Newcomb, the youngest. "State, Tech and A&M, more likely," Richard had sneered, laughing out loud, the first time he heard their names.

We're all glad to see one another. We always are. But the presence of Hilde and Bennie — or maybe it's just this many people — makes us all a little nervous. Pretty soon, Everest volunteers to build a fire and work on roasting the ducks, and I go with him.

"Nice catch you got," I tell him.

"Yeah. Good to have something besides fish for a change. Fish does get old."

His skin looks worse. His nose and cheeks, and the stretched skin on top of his head have a sick purple cast, like a bruise, like spoiled plums. A tracery of tiny veins shows hot red in it, and where they converge, the points are like pimples, tiny blood blisters. Two or three of those on his head are burst, little sores that glisten, scabs that have stayed tacky, never hardening.

"What're you doing?" he asks, not looking up.

I'm bending too close. "Does it hurt?"

"Hurt? What?" He's blowing on the fire.

"I don't know, my left big toe. Do those sores on your scalp hurt?"

"What difference would it make if they do?" He is looking up into my eyes now. "Yeah. They hurt like hell. Specially when I get salt water on them, which I do at least ten times a day."

"Well, why don't you wrap them in something? Or wear a hat?"

"Sure. I'm going to run around with my head wrapped up in a do-rag. I'll wear a rubber bathing cap when I go crabbing. Just as soon as I can find one. Leave off it, Juli. It don't matter. We all got our little aches and ailments, don't we? You think Jenny's teeth don't hurt her? What's she going to do? Run to the dentist? Just never mind it. Really, it's nothing. So what's been going on with you all?"

"I don't know. Nothing. Before today, when they came." Of course, there's Jaydie and me. I don't know if I can talk to Everest about it. We're not that close. And she and I haven't even . . . "Jaydie and I started sleeping together." It slips out on its own.

He looks up again and gives me his widest slow grin. "No shit. Well, that's wonderful, man."

"Well, not sleeping together, exactly . . . not living . . ." I squat down next to him. "I mean we just started to make love. The other day. Yesterday. I don't know what it means. Yet."

"Hm. What it means." Everest says, giving me a cuff on the shoulder and then throwing his arm around my shoulders and hugging me to him. "I figure you're old enough to know what it means. As much as anybody does. I mean, you been married, Juli."

"Hey, fuck you, Everest." I throw his arm off and shove away from him. "Go ahead. Get all excited because I'm sleeping with a woman. You can kiss my butt. Yeah, I was married, and I was also lovers with Richard for ten years, or did that slip your mind, you're so excited you think I'm finally normal."

Everest lays a chunk of wood on the fire, but not for emphasis. "Sit down, Juli." He's looking straight at me, steady-gazed Everest. "Just simmer down. It don't make me no difference who you make it with. I just thought you'd be happier to be with somebody. And I hate to be the one to remind you of it, but your pal Richard is long gone."

I'm acting like an asshole. "I'm sorry," I tell him. "You're right. I'm just . . . confused about it. Jaydie and I haven't even really talked about it yet, just done it."

"Never mind," he says, working on the fire some more. The fire is beginning to drop a glowing carpet of red coals. "But you and me are going to have to get along, bubba." He smiles at me. "Cause we're going to be close neighbours. We decided to move over here into town."

"Who?"

"Us, me and Jenny and the kids." He is obviously pleased.

"Oh yeah?" Oh, no.

"Yeah, we already brought some of our stuff with us today, and I guess later on me and Jenny are going to look around and decide which house to live in."

"Well, there's plenty of space, places to choose from," I

tell him, feeling the sky and the trees crashing down. It's not about Jenny and Everest. It just feels so frantic all of a sudden. I'm still trying to figure out what's happening with me and Jaydie and then all this . . . "Everest, I'll go get some plates and things. From the kitchen. I'll be back."

I'm hiding now, on the porch, where it turns around the west side of the house, where I can sit and watch the day fade out. If this crowd will let me. I'm cross-legged, back straight against the clapboard wall, breathing deeply, trying hard to be calm. I can hear bits of conversation, and the cries of the kids as they run back and forth in the yard, and the rub and scrape of the cabbage palms overhead. It's too much. I want to be running. Through the woods someplace, barefoot on a spongy carpet of moss and fern. I want drops of forest wetness brushing my face like kisses. I want to hear the rip of broad leaves parted by my chest as I race along, peaceful and wild and alone. Away from here. Like Richard. Richard is running through the woods someplace. Alone, and peaceful maybe.

Sylvia and Sophie Newcomb dance along below the porch, hand in hand, toward the back side of the house. Sophie Newcomb looks like she's enjoying herself, but Sylvia looks more like she's being dragged along. She must feel at least as overwhelmed as I do. But maybe having the other kids around, and the semblance of a social life, will be good for her. There isn't any other kind of therapy we can provide. It makes sense their moving over. Of course. It'll be all right, I guess. We could be friends, too, Everest and me, and Jenny, and Jaydie. We can surely help one another out. We won't have to be all on top of one another. I'll just need to remind myself to be calm sometimes. I don't need to run.

Like Richard. If Richard were alive to be running through the woods someplace tonight, he'd be barefoot. But the floor of the woods would be stinking swamp muck with bumps of hidden cypress root, lacerating stalks of saw palmetto, sand spurs bristling, and the jagged bits of civilization's shards slicing and stabbing his feet. He'd be shoeless for lack of choice. And he'd be running, not for the private joy, but to save that creamy hide of his from who knows what.

Jaydie comes around the corner of the porch, calling for Sylvia. "I wondered where you'd gone. Everest's going to have the ducks ready in a little while." She squats down facing me. "Are you all right?"

"I guess so. It's a lot of things happening, all at once."

"Isn't it?" she smiles tightly. "Juli . . . just . . . don't disappear? OK? It'll be fine. It'll probably be better, having more people. They're not a bad bunch, either." The little girls appear briefly from the back of the house. "Sylvia and Sophie, you go get cleaned up for supper now," she tells them. They freeze, as if her words have caught them, and then take off at a skipping run for the back of the house, giggling crazily. She turns back to me. "Just don't wander off. In the head. We need you. I need you." She puts her two hands on my shoulders.

"I need you too," I tell her. "I love you, I guess." There are tears in our eyes.

"You guess," she says, and I can see her eyes pulled between looking away and right at me, feel the impulses in her arm to draw me toward her and smack my face. She's grinning and crying.

"I do," I tell her, grinning and crying.

"Mom," Sylvia is shrieking. "Mom, somebody's coming!

Up the road!" She comes racing up onto the porch, her feet drumming along the wooden floor. Somebody else is coming!"

"That's real funny, Sylvia. OK, you and Sophie Newcomb need to get washed. We're going to eat in a few minutes. Ducks!"

"No, Mom!" she says urgently, tugging at Jaydie's hand. "Somebody's coming."

"She ain't fooling, Miss Jaydie," Sophie Newcomb says from down below. "It's really somebody coming down the road."

For the second time today we go around to the north side of the house, Jaydie and I gripping each other's hands, worried. Sure enough, a person is coming along the road, already on our side of the cut. In this light I can't make out the face. But there's no mistaking Richard's shock of silver hair, flying in the breeze like a white flag.

5

The long oblique wash of the setting sun colours Richard's face an unnatural red. And he doesn't look well. He is cross-legged on the porch floor, leaning back against the clapboard. There was a big flurry of amazed greeting when he arrived, but it's subsided as people have gone off to eat. Incredibly, we are alone. I'm perched on the porch rail facing him. I should probably be helping get Hilde and Bennie and Miss Audrey fed.

Richard didn't want to eat. He looks in a bad way. His skin is tight and transparent, his face giving out an unhealthy glow, above the straggly beard. There are rough patchy sores all over his arms, from the line across his biceps where a short-sleeved shirt would end, down to the backs of his hands. He has no energy. He's tired from travelling of course. But there's a stiffness in his body, not repose. Only his eyes are mobile. He's like a kid in an iron lung, clamped into place, all his child's energy beamed through his eyes. Slowly he flexes and points one foot at the ankle, and I watch his calf muscle contract into a knot under the pale skin of his leg. It's a cramped, pained movement. The only sound is the silvery rustle of the palms in the empty sky. Richard's eyes are bright, reflecting the sunset.

He doesn't eat, but I'm not going to insist. I don't know what's going on but I can't do anything to recreate our old status quo. And I don't really know how to say what's changed. He left. He took his chances. But he looks so bad. "Can't I get you anything?"

"No, I'm all right. Too tired to eat right now. Is there a bucket, or a pan? I want to go down and get some water, to wash my arms. It's been on my mind the whole way. I think salt water might help clear them up."

"Of course. You sit. I'll get you some."

"Besides," he smiles faintly. "You know, our vision of Cape Harrier as a watering hole."

"Still the clown."

"Still myself, I guess." He crinkles his eyes at me in a weak smile.

On my way back, from around the corner of the porch, I hear him talking and stoop to listen. "I didn't come back to be away from people, are you kidding? I was never more alone than in this last year. Oh, sometimes I would hang out with somebody, some group, for a while, travel together, try to cooperate. But you can't imagine how wary people are, Jaydie. It's not worth it. Whatever you get from trying to be together is more than lost by not knowing when the other person is going to split in the night, or eat your share, or steal your sneakers. And you know, I don't like to be alone. I never liked it. So I realized the best possible situation would be back here, if you guys were still around. No matter what, I knew we could just trust, be honest with one another."

"Simpler here, too," Jaydie says. "There's so few of us. Well, there were until today."

"That's not the point," he disagrees calmly. "Anyway I doubt it's going to stay like it is. There aren't many people out there, but most of them are moving all the time. Some of them are going to find their way down here sooner or later. For sure. Just that I thought the safest place to be was here."

"So you came back to be with us?"

He chuckles. "Yeah. And for the waters."

"Hm? Richard, um, things have changed some."

Suddenly I feel like a fool, eavesdropping in the twilight with a bucket and some clean rags in my hands. I turn the corner of the porch. I feel like dumping the bucket over his head. Instead I set it by him. "Here. Do you want me to wash your arms for you?"

"Thanks, Juli. No, I'd better do it. It's kind of delicate."

"It hurts a lot?" Jaydie asks.

"It feels like I've just been skinned," Richard says, dipping a rag into the bucket and squeezing it out. He doesn't have much grip. "I just have this feeling that salt water will help it heal. I guess you could say being able to do this has kept me going for the last month. All the way from Jacksonville. From what's left of Jacksonville."

"It always was a wasteland, if I remember right. But if it was salt water you were after, isn't Jacksonville still on the ocean? Have things changed that much?"

For just a second I can feel Richard flashing me a look that says, Shut the fuck up, asshole. And I know I'm babbling. I wish I would shut up. But instead he swallows and sighs and says quietly, "Juli. Juli. The idea of washing with salt water kept me going. But I came back to be with you." In the dark I can feel his eyes on me.

I came back to be with you. He's told me that before.

The first winter we were here, we closed up the inn and went down to Key West. For the warmth, but mainly to earn some cash so we could get the place together the way we wanted for the next season. I got a cooking job, Richard waited tables. We rented a room in a peeling old house on Simonton Street full of other seasonal transients, people who followed the tourists from Cape Cod and the Catskills in the summer to Sanibel and the Keys in the winter. We did make money, cooking and waiting. Richard made more than me, which made me jealous. He was an excellent waiter, breezy but unobtrusive. Also, he was turning tricks on the side. Some nights he wouldn't come home to the rented room. "I feel like it," he said, when I told him to stop. Or, "We're here to make a bunch of money, aren't we?" We did make a bunch of money. We left Key West with over $5000 clear, and a new engine in the Datsun, too. On the way back north we stopped in Miami. Richard dropped me at a restaurant supply house and I had an indulgent afternoon blowing money on kitchen equipment. "I need to get some shoes," he had said. While I was buying whisks and soufflé dishes, Richard went to Bal Harbour and dropped a grand on clothes he would never have reason to wear back here. Silk shirts, a mohair jacket, Italian loafers with the creamy texture of chocolate mousse. "I earned it," he told me. "At least that much I hustled myself." "Forget it, Richard," I said, when I saw what he'd done. "No, I don't care if you take them back. You'll need them because I'm leaving you here. Forget the whole thing. You'll need those clothes to earn your living here. I'm sure you'll do fine in Miami." "Julian," he reminded me, "it's my truck. You can't leave me here." "We'll split the money. What's left of it. I'll get one of my own. I've had it. I can't trust you. I think I'm afraid to be all the way out on Cape Harrier with no one to depend on beside you." He left me at the motel, and when he came back the next morning the thousand dollars worth of clothes weren't with him, but he had another few hundred in cash. "I came back to be with you," he told me. "I'm sorry. It was just something I felt like doing. Just something I felt I had to do. Forget it all, please. I need to be with you." I was unforgiving. He was solicitous. "I love you, Julian," he told me, wrapping his arms around me from behind and pulling me close, his fingers twining in the hair on my chest, tugging at it until it hurt.

"I came back to be with you," he says now, in the dark, holding the salty wet rag against a sore on his forearm without flinching. "With both of you. You were right, Juli. There's nothing out there. This is the best place to be now. Not because there's easy food and all that. But because there are you people I . . . love. You people I can trust."

You've said that before, I feel like saying. And did you stick around? But Jesus, I must be crazy. There were years in between, and plenty of changes around us. Can't I act like a grown-up around Richard? Can I act like a grown-up with Richard around? "Yes," I say, after a deep breath. "You can. Trust us."

"Of course you can," Jaydie says. What does she imagine is going on now in my head, or in his? "How does that feel," she asks him. "Any better?"

"It feels," Richard says, dropping the rag back into the pail and collapsing against the wall, "like a medieval torture. I'm . . . very tired."

"Of course," Jaydie says. "Let's get you to bed. Juli,

let's put Richard in your bed."

"Wait a minute," Richard says, low, pausing for focus. "I didn't come back and just expect . . . that we would be together . . . sleeping together, Julian. I realize . . . I left. I don't have any assumptions."

"Oh, that's all right," Jaydie begins, but I figure I'd better be the one to say it.

"Richard, things have changed here. Jaydie and I are lovers, sort of."

"Yeah." I can hear a faint smile in his voice. "I imagined you might be. That's nice."

"Sort of," Jaydie grumbles. "I'll murder you."

"Well, we haven't even talked about it at all," I say, hearing the whine in my voice. "We just started." I try explaining to Richard. She'll murder me. If she murdered Bullie, at least he deserved it. But that's insane. Of course she didn't. Though of course he did. And of course I won't. Deserve it, I mean.

We hold each other tight for a long moment, and then she rolls away onto her back. "OK then, let's talk about it. What do you want to say?"

"About what?"

"Don't play games now, Juli. About us. You seem to have some conversation in mind for us." Her tone is even, not sarcastic as the words suggest. "I guess you think we need to 'work things out' now that we're making love."

"Well." I can't seem to think what it is I thought we had to tell each other, to establish. I just draw a blank.

"I guess you think that everything's changed now," she continues slowly, evenly. "Because we went out on the island and made love. I'm not so sure. I think we've been walking circles around each other for a long time, avoiding . . . not sex . . . avoiding touch. Touching each other. Do you think . . . did you think that getting close would make it harder for us to get along?"

"No, I didn't think that. I don't think I ever imagined us getting close, any closer. Not becoming lovers, anyway." I can feel the tension in her body slacken. "Don't get me wrong, Jaydie. I depend on you. I've grown to, and I don't mind it. I like it. We've all got our weirdnesses . . . really, you have to laugh at this crew, don't you? . . . and both of us at least have a few strengths. And I've felt good enough . . . no, really good . . . about it being us, the two of us, handling things here. I never spent much time thinking past that. You seemed so . . . distant, protected behind your . . . competence. Behind I don't know what."

"While you've just been quietly sitting it out in your sunny corner," she says, her voice now shaded with emotion. "Since Richard left. Shut in. For the duration."

"Well, I can't remember this much conversation from you at one time in years, if you want to talk about shut in."

"Don't get defensive, Julian. Please don't waste time getting defensive. You were pining for him. Obsessed with him. Don't you think I could read you well enough to see that? Even Miss Audrey mentioned it to me now and then."

Oh god, psyched out by a batty Southern belle.

She rolls back to face me and slips her arms around my shoulders. "Is it going to be hard for you, now that he's back?"

"I don't know yet. He seems so subdued. I suppose I

figured he was dead. So it's hard to think I won't wake up tomorrow to find he never came back at all. Or that this whole day has been a dream. Not quite a nightmare."

"It wasn't a dream," she says. "They're all here, and Richard's probably right when he says they won't be the last to come either." Her voice is tight, catching. She sniffs, I realize she could be crying and brush her eyes with my open lips to confirm it. "I don't know why," she answers, though I haven't asked. "We're lucky. It could have been strangers. It's not the ones who came I have a problem with."

"Not even Richard?"

"Richard? He seems so pathetic, deflated. Richard's as welcome as anybody as far as I'm concerned. Maybe more, if it will make you happier to have him back. Will it?"

"I don't know. I told you. I guess I feel a little . . . cheated. I'd assumed that his leaving here had been a failure. Of his. I know this is disgusting but this is what I thought. But I felt good about that. Like I won. Even though I'd lost him . . . And now here he is back."

"But Juli," Jaydie whispers, "he has failed. He left, and couldn't stay away. He found out he couldn't live without you. You did win. If you want to talk about it like that. Richard's the prize. Sick, defeated Richard."

"Don't." I know I started it, but I roll away from her now, as if I could roll out of earshot.

"You're the one who was feeling cheated," she says anyway. "Funny. You'd think I might be feeling cheated, wouldn't you? Here I am finally getting next to this guy I've been watching and wondering about for years. Maybe a little happily-ever-after is about to happen here amid the ruins. And what happens next? His old boyfriend shows up the following day. If he weren't so ill I could almost imagine Richard timing it like this on purpose. That would fit, don't you think?"

She chuckles at her observation. We lie facing opposite dark walls. Now I realize, from the shaking of the mattress, that she is silently sobbing. Now I remember. "Jaydie," I whisper, laying my chin on her shoulder from behind. "Jaydie. What I wanted to talk about, before anybody came today. I wanted to talk about us, I wanted to tell you how glad I am, that we aren't just depending on each other's wits. We can touch each other. I wanted to say how much I hoped we could make a better life for each other. How making love made me feel suddenly so far out there . . . how totally, boringly alone I've been, and how glad I am now. I wanted . . . I wanted to say this and I wanted you to say the same things back. If I was a jerk about it, I guess I thought you wouldn't, or couldn't, or didn't want to. But I was wrong."

6

It's been three or four weeks. Things have settled down some. It's not that bad. It's really not that bad at all.

Bennie and Hilde moved back into their little house. I had the feeling she would rather have stayed up at Miss Audrey's. God knows, there's plenty of room. But Bennie insisted. It took a couple of days to get the place straightened up. Bennie kind of hopped around undoing things as Hilde and Jaydie got them done. Now the old people, Hilde and Bennie and Miss Audrey, spend most of their days rocking and swinging on the porch up at the big house. The cool weather has passed, so I yanked those shreds of old plastic down. It's a lot more cheerful for them without the plastic. Miss Audrey tunes in and out. When she's in, she and Bennie have these infuriating non-conversations. I guess they like to pull each other's chains. It works on me. The other day they were rocking away when out of nowhere Bennie announced, "Yep, we got great terms on the house. Took over an 8 per cent mortgage, practically nothing down . . . and the selling price? Don't even ask. What kind of a rate you got on this place, Audrey?" I have never heard anybody call Miss Audrey "Audrey".

"Yes, the Olivers were just the loveliest people you'd ever hope to meet," she came back. "And what a garden that Portia had. I used to look after the roses for her when they were back in Tallahassee."

"Porsche?" Bennie asked Hilde, incredulous. "What kind of a Porsche, with a garden?"

"The Olivers, Mrs Oliver," Hilde said quietly, trying I think to avoid Miss Audrey hearing. "The people from Tallahassee. From whom we bought the cottage."

"Yeh," Bennie went on, undaunted. "What a steal. So Audrey, when did you buy exactly? A long time ago . . . rates must have been rock bottom back then."

"This house has been in your family, no?" Hilde said, trying to put a better face on it.

"Not my family," Miss Audrey said. "The family of my second husband. Who were cotton factors in Appalachicola." This version of events is altogether new to me. But I long ago stopped trying to keep Miss Audrey's life straight. "They were quite successful in the years after the war. The grandfather — of my husband, that is — George Washington Euless, was elected to Congress. In those days, from Appalachicola, you took a boat along the coast to Cedar Keys, where you could get the train across Florida to Fernandina, and then go by ship to Washington, or Norfolk, Baltimore or wherever; I don't recall precisely what they did at that end. On one of his trips, he noticed this hill — as anyone would, since it's the only rise along this part of the coast — and eventually came back to build this house for when he retired. He was voted out finally, if you must know the truth."

"We looked in Cedar Keys," Bennie said. "There were a few places we considered. But Hilde thought it wouldn't be as peaceful. You were right, doll. You know, Audrey, she's got one hell of a head on her shoulders. It all looked the same to me."

"It's an Indian mound, actually," Miss Audrey drawled. "Not a natural hill at all. It does give a lovely view, though, doesn't it?"

"An onion mound?" Bennie turned to Hilde and said in a stage whisper, "An onion mound? What the hell is she talking about, onion mound? You know sometimes I wonder if anybody's upstairs there." He circled his index finger around his ear.

"What do you mean about the hill?" Hilde asked.

"Well, it was their dump, if you want to look at it truthfully," Miss Audrey said. "Which I always found amusing. Nothing but a big pile of oyster shells and rubbish. Thousands of years' refuse. Table scraps. I don't suppose it occurred to any of those feasting Indians what a trial all that lime would be to me in the garden. You couldn't count the truckloads of pine needless I've had hauled up here to try to get back some acid balance in this soil. Imagine! In this climate, having to struggle to establish azaleas."

"Indian? Ever find any artifacts in it?" Bennie asked, interest renewed.

"Indian artifacts? Oh, bits of pottery mostly. You ask Julian Heald. I believe he found a stone axehead once, putting in that little kumquat tree. You know Julian helps me with the garden now. Come to think of it. I must speak to him about another load cf pine mulch." All this time I had been below them in the garden and now fled to safety on the far side of the house.

Jenny spent a couple of days investigating every one of

the empty buildings in town. In the end, she settled on Macnamara's place, which was an obvious choice. With the exception of Miss Audrey's, it's the most impressive structure here. But a real mistake, in my opinion. It was designed in the days before anybody gave a thought to conservation and is completely dependent on electric power. No cross ventilation, a flat roof and no attic. It's built in some clammy industrial material called Ocala block that doesn't breathe, and has huge panels of sliding plate glass on its southern side. Not bad at this time of year, but without an overhang for shade the place is uninhabitable come May. Besides, that bad storm last summer took out a few of the glass doors. Jenny roped me into helping pull up the ruined carpet in the living room. Jenny, and Emory — who's fifteen, and the image of his mother, lean and sharp, but blond and freckled, with Everest's thin skin — and me. Before tugging Miss Jewell Macnamara's mildewed olive rug off the slimy concrete floor, I had no idea how much a damp shag rug could weigh. We had to stop, round up the other kids and Everest and Jaydie, who were at the dock shucking oysters, before we could get that mess out of there. My idea of living hell, insufferable torture, would be a cell padded with a mildewed olive-and-gold shag rug. Five minutes. Five minutes and I'd tell everything I knew. Sylvia and Sophie Newcomb tripped around giggling, trying to get the rest of us to roll them up in it. Well, Sophie tried, and Sylvia seemed to go along with her. Sylvia is doing a lot better since everybody came.

Richard seems better now, though he's weak. His arms are still raw. He's been washing them in sea water every day, and keeps his faith that this will help. "I think it was some chemical vapour. Something in the air. See the way it's only where my arms were exposed, out of short sleeves? Like a sunburn," he says. "I saw it on other people that way. Burns like this on their arms, legs, hands, on their faces. I became nervous about the sun pretty quick and always tried to keep my face shaded. Jesus. I can't imagine trying to talk, to blink even, if the skin on my face hurt as much as my arms do. Sometimes I just thank god for my vanity." With this new calmness I think Richard could say anything about himself, about me — without that old knifepoint sarcasm. But without the humour, maybe, too, and that's a loss. What he says just sits there now, small discrete stones placed deliberately on the path of a conversation.

We are in the canoe, having spent the morning setting crab traps. I'm paddling, and Richard lies facing me, propped back in the bow. It's midday, very still, with a strong spring sun. He is in long sleeves and jeans, and a hat. A pillowcase, torn-open, drapes from his hatbrim to shade his face.

"Now Everest's," he goes on. "That's skin cancer, I bet."

"Hm," I say. I try to fend off diagnostic talk. In all this time I've managed to avoid sharing medical hunches about anyone with anyone. But no doubt, Everest's condition is getting worse. Watching him over the weeks has been like watching the image on a photo come up, darken, and overdevelop, as if forgotten in its tray of chemicals. There are dark blotches the colour of prunes on his scalp and shoulders and arms. He bleeds a lot now, though he tries to keep us all from noticing. I don't know what he's worked out with Jenny; she goes through her days quietly, showing those bad teeth through a wan smile when you speak to her. I can't quite tell whether she's calm or distracted.

"I saw a lot of it," Richard goes on. "I was surprised that the rest of you here seem OK, so many people have it. It's an awful irony, isn't it, Juli? The most benign cancer, little sores the dermatologist pared off right away. Of all things to become an epidemic. I think something changed in the atmosphere, that ozone business or whatever it is, letting more infra-red through, ultra-violet, whichever. He's being remarkable though, Everest."

"He's a remarkable guy." I wonder if Everest can hear us talking about him across the water, where he and Jaydie have gone in the skiff to hunt ducks for perhaps the last time this season before they fly north. They're nearly out to Horseshoe, rowing, and every now and then a breeze from there brings the splash of their oars, a snatch of Jaydie's throaty laughter, Everest's resonant voice. Evidently they are enjoying each other. Well suited, both rock hard in their particular ways. They've been spending a lot of time together, hunting and things like that.

I steer the canoe into the shallow mouth of a tidal creek and draw my paddle up over the gunwales. Across the bay, sunlight flashes silver off the tin roofs of Cape Harrier, and out on Horseshoe and the other, nameless islands that are no more than sandbars, hammocks of scrub a foot or two above the tide, the fronds of the cabbage palms glint metallic as they shift and sway. When the rains come, moisture will hang in the air. The air will buzz with heat and weight, and every afternoon explode in a storm. And for six or seven months we will have plenty of fresh water. If we can still trust the sky.

"Steady us, can you Juli?" I thought Richard had only

leaned over to dip his arms in salt water again, but he is tugging at a clump of oysters that sticks its jagged edges out of the mud. "No, don't get out. I've got them." He drops it into the bottom of the canoe. "I fetched 'em," he declares, settling back onto his cushions, vinyl squishing on vinyl. "You fix 'em."

We swallow oysters, in turn. Richard draws the rag across his face to doze. The creek snakes away between low verges of marsh grass, toward low ridges of palmetto. The estuary is like a river delta in miniature. Like our miniature town, our shrunken world. I lean down into the canoe and listen to the hollow lap of water on the aluminium hull, the nudge of the keel on the soft bottom. I catch fragments of Everest and Jaydie across the water. They sound too animated, in the throes of hilarity, or some passion. They have been spending too much time together. Since our population boom, Jaydie has decided to wear clothes around town, around the others. But she still sheds them when she's out. What does she expect Everest to think, then? A red-blooded guy like him. Probably they are fucking right now on the damp splintery floor of the skiff, Everest's tight pink ass bouncing wide to the sky. No, it would be Jaydie on top. Yes, those would be the loud voices I caught, Jaydie's insistence, Everest low and steady and insistent too. He finds himself on his back, giddy with the random turning of the boat, her boney brown torso moving over him, huge and angled against an empty blue that offers no fixed referent. The yelps and cries are Jaydie's, rising, and Everest is silent, just his rushing breath between clenched jaws. Probably thinking about his family, and notions of loyalty and guilt, how he can have let himself do this to them, or to me.

A shot wakes me from sleep in the still heat of afternoon. Richard draws the pillowcase from his face and shrugs himself upright. "Duck soup," he murmurs. "A few more, Everest, so there'll be plenty to go around."

I guess I'm crazy. To even have imagined — oh, it's possible. Not likely, but not, on the other hand, ultimately any of my business. So who should I trust the least? Jaydie? Everest? Or myself?

"Bad dreams?" Richard is considering me as if I were a tangle of knots, looking for an end to pull.

"Uuh uuh." Of course, why shouldn't he be able to read me?

"I know this is hard for you, Juli, all of us descending here. I'm a little bit sorry I . . . no . . ." he shushes my motion. "I'm very glad I'm back here. I'm sorry when I think about how well the situation must have suited you, before. You're being very gracious and accepting. Which is lucky for all the rest of us since you're one of the few who's got some strength. But I know you don't like people around you that much."

"Look, Richard, I missed you very much. I told myself you were dead but I didn't know for sure and, anyway, you were very much alive in my head. You were a monster to me, in fact. I made you one. I wasn't calm, even if I might have looked it. I don't think it . . . I . . . would have let my relationship with Jaydie have much chance. In a funny way your coming home makes it possible."

"And, is it?" The new Richard: he asks because he wants to know, or to help talk it through maybe, not to wheedle. "Are you calmer?"

"I don't know. Look." A reddish egret has come to feed in the shallows ten yards from us. She stands motionless on stick legs, peering at a sharp angle into the water. Suddenly she bursts into dance, running along with wings flapping, casting shadows and ripples into the water that will attract her prey, changing direction abruptly like something possessed. "I think the situation is better for us, though. She and I can be lovers without having to get everything from each other. It's like being members of a normal community. That sounds funny. It may not be normal, but at least we're not completely alone together. She's friends with Everest, with Hilde. I don't think I'm any less crazy myself." Can I give him a for instance? Can I say, Only now I was imagining her two-timing me with Everest in that boat. "Oh, it's more trouble working things out with a larger group of people, and so many of them not being very well. The everyday things. I miss that feeling I used to have that this was the end, the edge of civilization, of survival. It was very seductive to me, that emptiness. It's a little less zen now. You can almost imagine a future, generations, mundane normal things like seasons and gardens and mending crabtraps and figuring out how to weave. Not that I'm thinking much about the future. Yeah, I don't like people around me that much. I love having you back though."

"You do." He's not asking.

Do I? "We know each other so well, I mean. Just talking like this."

"Yeah."

The egret makes another wild splashing run, freezes, and then punctures the water with her hard darting beak.

Success. "What about you, Richard? Being alone."

"I'm not alone. I'm not lonely." Affectionately, he puts the sole of his foot against my calf. "Sex? For the time being I can't stand being touched anyway. If this stuff ever clears up I'll consider corrupting Emory. I think I've grown up enough to take a turn at corrupting an innocent manchild, don't you? He's a little hunk-and-a-half, or have you stopped noticing that sort of thing?" He gives my leg a gentle kick.

"Well, what a relief to hear some trace of your former self."

"Oh, never fear, Julian. Richard is enduring as the ages."

We paddle quietly back on the flat, tea-coloured bay, Richard facing front and helping now. There is another shot. Another shell spent, hopefully another duck. Three feet underwater, the canoe's shadow follows us across the dwarfed sand-ridge topography. Purple shells dot the bottom, beauty spots on a perfect complexion. Like lesions. Far to our left, its foreshortened silhouette indistinct against the low green blur of Horseshoe Island, the rowboat is also heading back toward town. The long rays of the afternoon sun ring against the surface like a hammer striking copper.

We've waited around a long time on the porch for Everest and Jaydie. The sun is almost down, the intricate twisting limbs of the big live oak and the whisps of hanging moss black against the western sky. Finally Jaydie comes dragging up the path, alone, emptyhanded.

She hesitates at the edge of the yard, looking to see which of us are here, I guess. "My, you took a while," Miss

Audrey calls, from the swing. I look up and see Hilde there too. I say, "Hey, babe, Everest down cleaning the ducks?" actually trying to determine whether to get a fire going or what we will have for supper. Jaydie approaches and from my perch on the top step I can see her face tensed, cramped up around the eyes. She brushes past me before I make the connections to ask the obvious question — "What's wrong?" — and goes straight to the two old women. I can see Miss Audrey's and Hilde's faces, highlighted in the sunset. Miss Audrey examines Jaydie for a long minute, and her flabby expressionless moon-face twitches and pulls taut. She sits up straight and takes one of Jaydie's hands in hers. "Something has happened, now, Jane Deale, hasn't it," she says, agreeing to the fact more than asking. And Jaydie says, in the smallest voice I've heard, "Everest shot himself, Miss Audrey. Everest killed himself on Horseshoe."

Hilde's hand goes to her mouth and traps a little cry, her forearm pale and blank where I am always expecting to see those tattooed numbers, and she slumps back, setting the swing in motion. But Miss Audrey sits up stiffer and holds onto Jaydie, so it swings skewed, creaking its chains. Richard is lying down on the porch floor behind me, and I'd thought he was asleep, but I hear him whisper, "Oh my god," and then he is up, approaching Jaydie, laying a hand on her shoulder and asking her to tell what had happened. Only I remain still, stunned to silence by the news, and then flooded with shame. But it doesn't really matter how I react. I'm not the focus of anyone's attention. Only Richard's, briefly. "I'll go after Jenny," he volunteers, and I know he'll do the hard job of giving her the news. As he passes he gives me this peeved questioning look. It makes me wonder who the strong ones among us really are.

7

We are shocked to immobility by this horrible news. The porch swing continues its erratic course, in ever shorter curves, until it just dangles. Miss Audrey keeps hold of Jaydie's wrist. "I tried to stop him, Miss Audrey. He said he couldn't stand the pain." There's no great emotion in it. But she must be exhausted. To row that heavy skiff all the way from Horseshoe singlehanded, at the end of the day in the sun. "He was bleeding like, oozing from all those sores. I don't know how he kept us from realizing how bad it was. He said his life was dripping away through those sores. He said he had bitten his tongue bloody, not to scream with the pain." She says these terrible things slowly, with anaesthetic dullness.

Hilde murmurs, "I go now to see after Bennie." She pauses to touch Jaydie's arm for a moment on her way to the steps. "Sit down, dear," Miss Audrey says, guiding the passive Jaydie around to Hilde's spot on the swing. This awful news has knocked us into a stupor. Me, anyway. I am still on the step where I have been since before Jaydie got back, watching the scene as if from very far away. Wishing I were very far away, and alone.

In a little while Richard comes back, leading Jenny by

the hand. Jenny seems fine at first, composed. Jaydie gets up, takes a few steps toward her, says her name, and Jenny collapses against her. She hangs on Jaydie's shoulders sobbing. Jaydie stands there supporting her, looking barely involved. The last little daylight is going now. Way out over the Gulf I watch a low crimson smear of it drain pale and then evaporate. All the quiet sunsets since I came to this place, all the placid coral dusks that take so exquisitely long to disappear into the mirror of the sea.

"On our way out to the island, I asked him if it hurt," Jaydie says wearily, heavily, when Jenny has calmed enough to listen. "He started talking about the pain. It was getting worse, he said. He hadn't been able to sleep. He said he could hardly keep from screaming all the time."

"I knew he couldn't sleep," Jenny mumbles, sobbing. "But I asked him every day if he was hurting."

Jaydie stands back a little from her, silent, somewhere else. I am suddenly afraid she is going to leave us, retreat behind that mute fastness where she used to hide. She's been so very present these last weeks, since everybody came — engaged, and giving. Come back, Jaydie. Jenny cries, "I asked him that, Jaydie. Why did he always tell me no?" I hear my own voice saying, "Come back, Jaydie."

For a minute she looks like she is actually debating the idea. "He couldn't stand not to be strong for you," she says finally to Jenny. "The kids. He couldn't stand to let us all down." Hasn't he let us down now? Wouldn't the inevitablity of his death have let us down soon enough? Jaydie is choking up. I'm on my feet going toward her and I can see the tears on her face. I'm crying now myself. But she stops me with a shake of her head, a shrug that says to stand aside. Her long hair falls stiff, hanging lifeless at her shoulders as she moves her head. Her hair used to look so nice, in the old days. Full and light and natural-looking. She wore it in the perfect cut for a place like this, an easy layered cut that always looked great whether it was windy or she'd just come from swimming and the ends were curling up with dampness. She would come downstairs to the bar after showering and use the spread fingers of both hands to fluff it out as it dried. It would give off a herbal whiff of conditioner you could catch above the tobacco and the beer.

"Once he started talking about it he couldn't stop. He was crazy with the pain. But, Jenny, don't make me tell it all."

I could cut it for her. Maybe it would get her back that ease. But of course we have no shampoo, nothing to wash away the years' deposits of salt water minerals, secretions of scalp oil, nothing to put back what's been leached by time and sun and the poisoned sky. Wouldn't we all look nice with a haircut, feel fresh after a shower and shampoo? Jenny's black hair parted in the centre and braided, or teased up, rounding out her long, sharp face. Richard's fine silver hair floating around his head like an aura. Even I would feel better. Even I would use a mirror again. I guess I can be as self-absorbed as anyone.

"Yes, you tell it all," Jenny insists.

Richard sits on the porch rail facing them; I am leaning against it with my thighs, facing away into the darkness. Now he reaches an arm across the space between us and lays his hand on my shoulder. This is a request — that I look at him, or that I turn around, that

I come back myself. He knows me so well.

"He wasn't planning to do it. "I'm sure," Jaydie says.

"How could he have been planning it? We was just talking this morning about where to put a garden. That's plans."

"Look. Once he got started about how much it hurt he just couldn't stop. He was moaning and jumping around — I thought he was going to turn the boat over. You didn't see how bad the pain was. He must have done everything he could to keep it from you." She sits down again next to Miss Audrey. "He calmed down some and we went on to the island. I still had no idea — he still had no idea, I'm sure." She stops talking. I think she is crying again. "Shit, Jenny. I can't explain it to you." Her voice is stretched, distorted. "I lost him as much as you lost him. We've all lost him."

"He wasn't your husband," Jenny says, standing over her. But there isn't any resentment in it, just her statement of the fact. "I'm not asking you to explain anything. I just have a right to know how he went." She has put out her hand, is touching Jaydie's brow. "I didn't have to watch it, Jaydie. I'm sorry you did. But you have to tell me."

Hilde has come back up on the porch, come to stand between Richard and me at the railing. Her breathing is rapid and shallow, moist with emotion. I feel contact must be made with her, that she needs some release. "This is terrible, isn't it?" I offer lamely.

"I'm so frightened."

How rapidly she had recognized Everest's place in this economy of survival of ours. Poor Hilde, she must have felt so relieved to make it back here and find us managing so well, and now this. She's right to worry. No one else among us had Everest's skills as a hunter, his knowledge of the swamp and these waters. She had grasped his role much faster than I ever did. With me it took years. I had to get over my suspicions, my fears of him — my asusmptions that because we came from such different backgrounds, lived such different lives, that he would judge me, reflexively, negatively. As what? An outsider, urban and intellectual, soft and helpless, as a faggot. That he would take in the gingerbread woodwork on the inn's porch, painted lavender and cream, the European cars of our clientele, and see us as alien, as a threat. That if he knew that when I cooked fish in the kitchen of that adorable old building I might do it any way in the world but breaded and deep fried; it would turn his stomach. But of course all of those images came from inside me, not from him. Most likely he had his own notions of how I judged him inferior. I could imagine the particulars, but what's the point? We weren't ever close enough to have talked about it. We probably never would have been. "Yeah, it's going to be hard to fill his place. We all depended on him for so much."

"There are lots of things I wish I'd had him teach me," Richard adds.

"No," she says. "Yes. But it is Bennie. He is dying also. Not just now, but soon he will die. Yes, I know it. He is very sick, and I have nothing to heal him. And when he dies, I think I can't go on myself." In the background, Jaydie is telling how Everest blew himself away: stumbl-ed, shot, missed, birds breaking cover in outrage.

"Don't say that, Hilde," Richard says.

"No, I maybe can't. All these years I have been with just

him, no children and no family, after I lost all my family in Germany. Many times I felt I can't go on, and always Bennie jokes with me and reasons with me. He is my engine."

"Hilde," Richard says, "you have tremendous strength. Please . . ."

"Perhaps. But without him I feel I can't move. And I begin to think, Why should I? Oh, you maybe see Bennie as just a fool. And he is a fool, and a child. You see me humouring him, taking care of him. But that is not who he is to me. That you maybe don't see."

"Hilde, you're so used to taking care of him that you can't imagine not having to." I can tell that Richard is angry now. "Yes, if he dies it will change your life, it will be hard for you. But you don't have the right to talk about not going on. Even Everest didn't, I don't think. But anyway, you're well, and we need you. We'll be your family." Jaydie is saying: . . . got up, turned the shotgun on his head. Then out loud, "His arm was barely long enough to aim it at himself." And she pleads, "Look, Jenny, this is his blood on me, here. And here." I'm having trouble listening to all this at once. "Richard, calm down," I say, meaning, I can't hear.

"Shut the fuck up, Julian," he hisses. "What is this obsession with calmness? Some other day, maybe. Right now is not the time to worry about that. You're out of your mind."

And then, he is crying. "I'm sorry," he says. "But it's true, I mean what I said. There isn't any calmness."

"Never mind, never mind," Hilde says to us both. I move to hug him, and he yelps with the pain of being touched, and laughs at himself, and goes on crying. Now I guess every one of us is crying. Jaydie keeps repeating, "I've got his blood all over me," and Jenny, when she realizes that the kids have all come into the yard, stands and wails. She stands with her arms hanging helpless at her sides and her face wide open in terror or shock as if the thing is right in front of her, Everest blown apart, as if transfixed. Richard goes down to the kids, and after a minute Hilde follows him.

And then Miss Audrey is calling, commanding. "Jenny. Jenny Thibault!" She says sharply. "You listen to me for one minute now. You just don't know." Her voice is clear and strong, without that excessive southern languor, unaccented practically. Jenny is surprised into attention, as are we all. "You don't know why people do the things they just have to do," Miss Audrey tells her. "Things have gone so you just don't know what to expect. Everest was a fine boy and you're going to have a hard time without him. If you were going to go ahead and start asking to know why, why did he have to do it, you'd best stop right now before you get started. You need an answer to that? He was in pain. That's what Jane is telling us and that's all we'll ever come to know on the matter. I'm sorry, sugar. That doesn't make it hurt any less. But it will make it stop hurting sooner. You listen to me now."

Things have gone. Everest is gone. Richard came back. Bennie is going, and now Miss Audrey is right here, lucid and in touch. Can it be that she always has been? In the darkness, in the moment when she stops speaking, we can hear one another stifling our grief.

If I slept at all last night I don't remember; I'm not rested.

Jaydie finally came to bed, after sitting up with Jenny. She fell into a sprawling, twitching sleep. She always sprawls, but this time she was heavy as a fallen tree, flailing at things in her dreams. She was nowhere near me, and never sought my touch. My own tossing never disturbed her, and she didn't know it when I got up with the first light.

I can't get this thing about what really went down between her and Everest out of my mind. I wish I could just accept what she says. But I guess I suspect that it was actually Jaydie who pulled the trigger. That even after he decided he had to kill himself, Everest couldn't bring himself to do it. That after they'd argued about whether he could stand to live any longer with the pain, his demand that she do it for him was what they fought about. In the boat. Or no, maybe it wasn't until they stood in the muck and jumble of mangrove roots that edges the lagoon, and Everest realized the awkwardness of reaching the trigger of the long-barrelled shotgun with his own hand, of pushing the wrong way against its tension spring, after he had sent one load of shot off into nowhere, raising a storm of ducks and pelicans, that he demanded and finally convinced her to do it for him. I have this picture of them tripping around on the mangrove roots after each other, slipping, wrestling, their bodies getting covered with mud. Why can't I just believe her? I want to put my two hands on her shoulders and sit us down and ask. Or I might get the answer I want just as easily by asking her straight out how Bullie died. I feel these questions, this question, physically, foaming up in me, filling my chest. I feel like I have to sit on my own rib cage to hold it in.

Actually I am sitting on our dock in the bay, watching the sun rise up over the burned out scrub on the far shore. My legs hang over, and my bare feet rest on the gunwale of the rowboat. Each slight swell raises and lowers my knees. The water moves up and back in the salt grass and flotsam of the shoreline with a peaceful sound, like breathing.

I climb the path back to the house, hauling the pail of sea-water Richard will need to wash his arms. Here is Jenny standing at the porch rail, looking out to Horseshoe. "I'm fixing to get his body back," she tells me. Last night, admonished by Miss Audrey, she had seemed meek, reduced. But now she shows a haggard bloodshot resolve. "Well look, Jenny. It's so early. Sit down. Did you eat? We'll wait until the others are up." Now I have a picture of the coming day — Richard and Jaydie and me rowing out to the island to collect Everest's remains — that is making me weary in advance. But later, when Jaydie and the kids appear, it turns out that Jenny is intending to go herself. "I'm coming with you, Mama," Emory announces. "You can't row all the way out there and back by yourself." Auburn says, "I'm coming too." And Jenny begins to agree.

Jaydie hears this and says quietly. "No." Jenny and her boys are getting up to move off. "You better bring a jug of drinking water along, Auburn," she is saying. "And we better bring something to eat. Ask Julian if you can get some pecans."

Jaydie says again, "No. Julian, she can't take them out there."

"I figured we would go," I tell her. "You and me, maybe Richard."

"Jenny," she says, taking Jenny's hand in both of hers. "Listen, he turned a shotgun to his own head. Don't take the boys with you." She doesn't want to tell it in front of the kids. She doesn't want to tell it again. She is beginning to cry.

"Well, maybe so, but Emory's right, Jaydie, I can't go by myself."

"Just don't take the kids."

Jenny goes to Auburn, puts an arm on his shoulder, and takes the plastic water jug from him. I make a move toward the house, to wake Richard. "You come then, Jaydie," Jenny says. "You and Hilde."

"I'm coming, Mama," Emory insists.

"Emory, listen," Jaydie forces herself to say. "You really don't need to. Your dad is . . . got messed up pretty bad. Just . . . trust me that you shouldn't go."

"No! It's none of your business. Mama, I'm coming."

"Emory," Jenny says, "you go ask Miss Hilde if she'll come to the island with Jaydie and me."

The kid is crying now and hates the indignity of this. "No," he yells. "I won't either. It's none of their damn business." He runs off to the back of the house, but not so fast that we can't still hear his cries receding.

"Really," Jaydie starts to say to Jenny, "it's better."

"Oh, you're right," Jenny sighs. "Will someone just go after Hilde? No, I'll go. I want us to get on with it now."

So Richard and I are left, with the kids. Bennie never gets up. Hilde asks me, with a sort of helpless shrug, to go down and look in on him once in a while. Miss Audrey doesn't get up either. It's as if she is completely spent after her brief clarity last night. When I carried her to the outhouse she never spoke, never registered my presence.

She just whimpered once when I set her back in her bed.

The kids are pretty subdued too. I'm not much good at raising their spirits. Richard's better at it, engaging and cajoling, wheedling responses and occasional half-grins, Richard of the highly developed social skills. Really he is very good with the kids. But I get the feeling through all this that Richard is at pains to keep his distance from me. For so long I was so angry at him. Then when he came back here broken — changed, subdued — that just seemed irrelevant. We've been pretty warm with each other, but there is still some unfinished business between us, I guess. A fight, or an all-night talk, or maybe just the rest of our lives rubbing each other the wrong way, getting on each other's nerves, here in this place. What a time to think about it. Still, I wonder if we will ever make love again. I suppose I'd like to. Not so much because I desire him sexually as that I am curious to do again something I have done so many times. Touch again what was so familiar, and be touched.

When Emory comes back, abashed, Richard tells him he ought to get into the habit of wearing a hat. "I don't have a hat," Emory says. So the two of them spend the morning making hats for everybody, out of LP covers that Auburn produces from the Macnamara boys' playroom. They cut oval holes in them so they sit down low on our brows like squashed mortarboards. The girls like them especially, and decorate theirs with veils of Spanish moss along the fronts. Richard wears his tilted, with a corner pointing to the front. Always the rake. It is like a Three Stooges graduation day. Only the students are barely literate. But somehow reading skills don't strike me as useful in the world they are entering. You young people are the future of our nation and you will look back on this day et cetera. Or anyway the future of eds of the culture one. I guess we ought to put some thought into what we can teach them. We ought to try to remember what we can of Everest's useful knowledge, for example, before we forget it in the lethargy of summertime. We ought to think ahead, make some plans. It's not that I want to. But it would be a good idea. But what is our responsibility? To preserve some shreds of the culture for future generations? Those random paperbacks that remain and a halting ability to decipher them? Or merely to preserve our selves, our bodies, our children, their children? The thought that this little clutch of nestlings will inevitably beget more makes me want to gag. Who will do it with whom? Well, one of the boys and Sylvia, since the tabu on incest should be preserved, and though he'd be more interested in the boys, perhaps Richard with Sophie Newcomb . . . no, I really have to stop this right now.

Auburn has climbed into the live oak with his orange — I handed out oranges, almost the last of them for this year, but it seemed appropriate. He sits high above us tossing bits of peel down on Sophie Newcomb. "Quit," she says. "OK," he says, tossing another bit of peel, which lands thunk on the ledge of Sylvia's album-cover hat and bounces to the ground in front of her. Sylvia sits very still under this barrage, and slowly her face twists up in tears. "Quit it," she wails. "Auburn!" Sophie turns her head up to her brother and commands, "Auburn, quit!"

"Auburn," Richard says firmly. "Not today, all right? Everybody is feeling kind of edgy today and we need to treat one another a little gently."

"OK," Auburn says. "Richard! I can see a boat."

"It's your mom and them."

"No. Way past the island. A sailboat. With red sails."

"You do not," Emory says.

"I ain't shittin, Emory."

"You do not either," Emory says, mounting the live oak with ease. "Hey," he yells. It is. A sailboat with red sails."

Everybody jumps up to climb the tree for a look, and a lot of album-cover hats falls to the ground. The boys shinny up a branch and leap off onto the porch roof. In a minute they are straddling the high peak of the house's tin roof. Richard and Sophie climb ahead, but Sylvia is wary at the base of the tree, not knowing quite how to go up it. Snuffling, rubbing her eyes, she turns and looks up at me.

"Need a hand?" I ask her.

"I'm scared, Juli,"

Probably she is scared of who might be on the boat, but why not get her to conquer the little fear of climbing trees? I'm scared of who might be on the boat myself, when it comes to that. "It's OK kid. I'll be right behind you. Here, I'll lift you up and you grab that first branch. That's it. You got it." She hasn't, really. She never makes it higher than the first branch.

We spend the midday aloft. The boat is far out, drifting across our horizon. I can only barely make it out, but the others see it better and they say it has two red sails and a spinnaker. Whoever it is must not realize we are here. Which could be just as well. What I do see, far to the west above the Gulf, is a grey haze that coalesces into gently rising billows of cloud as the day wears along. Nothing will come of it today. But it won't be many weeks before the storms start, the hard china blue of the sky closed in by thick clouds of blinding white that turn grey, and then black, as they shut out the sun and suffuse this panorama with a sick-green glow before the lightning starts.

8

Sylvia has my hand in hers, smiling expectantly from my face to Jaydie's and back. "I can come too?" I need to tell her no without hurting her feelings. I need to establish communication with this kid that goes beyond our habit of grunted bare responses. I glance to Jaydie for help but she doesn't meet my eyes. She's looking at Sylvia, a tentative smile at the corners of her mouth which is probably self-protection in case I blow it. So this is a test. I try touch, squeezing Sylvia's hand and patting her shoulder. "No, kiddo, you can't come. Your mom and I have been promising each other a day alone. Besides, we'll be gone a long time and what if you got tired of walking?" It seems OK, she doesn't seem crushed. "Then we'd have to carry you which I hope I never have to do again, you're getting too big for that. Some other time. Maybe tomorrow." All right, Julian. Shut up already. But "kiddo"? I don't know if kiddo is going to work with Sylvia. Although she has definitely lightened up lately.

"You can so carry me. I'm not that big either." Sylvia says, trotting off, as if she never wanted to come anyway. "Bring me something, then." A pair of trainers. That's what I'd like to bring her, with all the running around she does.

We go down the path to the dock and turn left, up the narrow ragged beach that skirts the bay. Incredibly, in this backwater that never had an industry more advanced than subsistence fishing — incredibly, after these last years of desolation — this beach is as trashed up as the shoulder of a freeway, junky as a cracker shack's front yard. It is patches of mud and sand crossed with driftwood stumps, with fallen palms that decay to the texture of shredded wheat, with unidentifiable twists of rusting metal. Sunk in to their gunwales are the hulks of boats that have yet to finish rotting, plastic jugs and useless tangles of yellow nylon rope that never will. The shards of a big terracotta sewer pipe that once dumped Cape Harrier's sludge into the bay cut a gash right across the sand, as the tides slowly, slowly dissolve them. One day there will be just a straight, shallow seam of alien red clay. Walking along behind Jaydie with my eyes down, I half expect to look up and see six or eight old cars, faded Chevettes, big Mercurys, up on blocks, with their hoods gaping, engine parts strewn around like the fish guts the guys used to fling up here as they cleaned the morning catch. What shells there are on this strand are brittle and drab, a litter of jagged oysters, occasional thick sea clams or broken whelks bleached white, heavy and gritty and porous as chunks of limestone. Once I found a lightning whelk that still had colour, a small one that must have only just died, its translucent pattern of beige and slate-blue intricate and subtle as weaving. It was like a visitation, a small miracle, some small pulsing animal in the palm of my hand. That's how rare it was. As we walk, we startle the shorebirds who feed in the sedges and mud flats. They are abundant as ever, and more wary, so much less used to people now. I recognize the herons and egrets and the white ibis, with their long hot-pink beaks, that travel in loose fluttering lines like bleached linen against the sky. But I can never tell the others apart. I'm at a total loss with these scores of nervous waders and darters who fly off shrieking before us with split-second flashes of white and black wing. Turnstones, maybe, oystercatchers. All the indistinguishable sandpipers: buff-breasted, spotted, solitary, least.

I follow Jaydie, the two of us walking quietly up the beach. She unwraps the sarong from her hips, stuffs it into a sack that hangs from her waistband against one hip. That knife in its sheath gently slaps the other. Her ass and thighs are tanned and sinewy, stretching and contracting in the rhythm of her walk. It's nice to walk along behind her like this to consider her body, her person, privately. It's nice to walk along behind her, as if we could go on walking indefinitely.

She stops to bend and pick a handful of beach peas. These ephemeral legumes of ours — their frail vines carry a spotting of colourless blossoms and a few matured pods at the same time. The season of their blooming and fruiting is just now, a moment in the spring. They are delicate as snow peas, crispy, thin as paper, sweet and nourishing in an infinitesimal way.

"Thanks, Jaydie." I munch a mouthful. "If only we could plant them. Grow them for ourselves."

She picks a few more ripe ones, and I can see her wavering, hand at the mouth of her sack, over whether to eat them now or bring them back. "Eat them, babe. There're so few. We'll get the kids to go out and pick some more. You eat those."

Jaydie smiles as she chomps up the pods. "What would we do — eat nothing but beach peas for ten days a year? They're always gone so fast." Is she taking me seriously?

For some reason, I have a very distinct picture in my mind: the breeding of peas. "Maybe we'd be able to train them. That's not what I mean. Find the . . . what is it? . . . recessive traits. Genes. For when they ripen. For size. Maybe we could domesticate them. Breed them. As a staple crop." I can see pea plants in rows, staked, against a stone wall. Where is this scene? We don't have stones on the Gulf coast, much less stone walls. A garden's paths, the sound of wooden cart wheels, bells pealing. Of course. Gregor Mendel, in Germany somewhere. This is silly. Domesticating wild peas can't be as easy, as picturesque, as a one-paragraph anecdote in a high school biology text. Probably took him a lifetime, and he wasn't looking to his crops for sustenance, either. "But why not?" I can see clipboards and tedious noted observations, carefully hoarded stashes of seed. Bushels of dried peas in rough burlap bags stacked high in metal warehouses. Split pea soups. Peameal breads. A rejuvenated civilization based on domestication of the beach pea.

"Gregor Mendel," she says over her shoulder, proceeding down the beach. "School lunches. Number ten cans of revolting squishy peas. Do you remember the smell of peas in the cafeteria on winter days? I always wanted to puke. You're not going to take us back to all that, are you?"

"Do you want to end up with a diet of 90 per cent raw oysters, then? I don't think our sex life could take it."

"I'm willing to try, big boy. What about you?"

"You talk a good game, Miss Deale." But I'm thinking about the dish that was my signature at the inn — oysters baked in a loaf, layered with spinach and breadcrumbs and mushrooms. In season, the spinach came from my own garden. Could I use ground dried peas in place of the breadcrumbs? But without mushrooms? There are wild ones, but we're afraid to eat them, and have no way of finding out which are safe.

Jaydie stops suddenly, whirling in her tracks, one hand swinging up to grab my shoulder. "I'm not playing, Julian." Her eyes, deep and grey, fix on mine.

"I'm not either. I don't blame you for anything, Jaydie. I really think we should, uh . . ." — she's still staring hard — "breed peas. Did I ever tell you I love you?"

"If you did, I don't recall. So it couldn't have been recently enough. And I believe the word you're looking for is 'husband'."

"Is this a proposal? Some kind of proposition?"

"Julian, honey," she says, plodding along the sand again. "We're way beyond proposals."

"You mean this is something we can depend on."

"Well, I'm not going anywhere."

We fall quiet, walking along the shore to where the bay narrows, until we are at the mouth of the little river. We can wade across, easy going most of the way in the slow muddy current. Our bare feet slide and paw in the silky muck of the bottom. The water is a nice temperature, and the day has warmed up, so it's refreshing to be waist deep in the flow. Only that I think about alligators for the few minutes we are crossing the deepest place, in the middle, farthest from the safety of either shore; with the water at our shoulders and our arms extended, holding our clothes. They're not particularly common. It's just this more or less irrational fear, I guess. I did see one near here once — a sow with her litter of cute twelve-inch babies which all leapt off the bank in a round of splashes as I approached, green and scaly and seemingly harmless as frogs.

We stand dripping on the east bank. "It doesn't look any different to me. From here." We never have seen the results of that fire.

"No," she agrees, stepping into the woods beyond the bank. "Not any more. It was eerie, though, right afterwards." A surprise to me. "I was here one day, with Everest." Jaydie's voice catches on Everest's name, like a hiccup. But none of us has had that much chance to utter it. None of us has recovered. Jenny swings between helpless self-pity and dead silent, apparent competence. I don't know what's really going on with her. Maybe she's withdrawing too far. I wonder how long it will be before any of us can talk about Everest without pain, consider his suicide, the meaning of his loss. If I could get my hands on him now I'd just as soon wring his neck. Jaydie says, "The fire raced through so fast — everything was so dry — that it left the trees pretty much alone. Just the scrub, on the ground. The ground was covered with grey ash. The tree trunks were singed, the palm fronds a little, the lower ones. But it was all the stuff on the ground that had burned away. The vines and creepers. Grey ash everywhere, that puffed up in little slow clouds every time you took a step. Soft, light clouds of ash. Just how I always pictured walking on the moon. But the eerie part was that the woods were still perfectly alive, over our heads." Now — what? a month? two months later? — the ash has been washed into the sandy ground, colouring it a little darker than it would normally be. The fresh floor is cleared out, freed of bushes and tangles and, beneath the pillars of tree trunks, is as open as a gallery. There are brilliant green shoots of new scrub everywhere. And overhead, a healthy canopy of pine and cypress and cabbage palm. Only the black scars around the bases of the trees say "fire".

We put down our things and go to cut some swamp cabbage. Jaydie uses the big knife to chop down half a dozen young palms, and we sit down to peel off the woody layers that cover their sweet, nutty hearts. One we eat; the rest go into Jaydie's sack to be carried home. There are no outings solely for pleasure, no whole days when we don't pay some attention to survival.

From the sack, Jaydie takes a sheet. She spreads it out, and we lay down together. The sunlight falls in pieces on our naked bodies, on the forest floor. Above our heads, the palm fronds sigh and shimmer. We doze off.

In half-consciousness, we make love to each other, in fits and starts, in starts and stops. We hover, we float above that place where energy, wakefulness, turns to balance, to satisfaction, turns to sleep. For a long time neither of us comes, because we are not doing this to get to that, not working ourselves up to anything, but simply doing it, to stay afloat. We have a lifetime of time for this. I do come, once, smoothly, slickly, without peaks and catches, without interrupting the drift. Jaydie comes too, maybe, maybe more than once, like tantric breathing, like a tingling flow of released deep breath.

In my dream I hear her talking. Juli, I'm scared, she

seems to say. In my dream there is a caravan of buses on the road into town, but the buses have spinnakers like sailboats, and the sails are really jelly fish, billowing. Those round jelly fish called cannonballs, purple and glowing and soft.

"Juli, I'm scared," she murmurs. "Wake up. I have to tell you something."

She's leaning up on one elbow, looking down into my face. Not alarmed, though. Does she mean she wants to play that game — ritual, exercise, whatever it was — we used to fall back on when we each needed the other's concentration? It seems so inappropriate now. Not embarrassing — this is just the two of us, way out here in the woods. But unnecessary. I think we can reach each other without the artifice.

"What's wrong, Jaydie?"

"I'm pregnant."

Above her head, blue sky. The ragged stubble of a palm frond with charred tips, a ragged crown of cypress. That hard blue sky. "How do you know?"

"Of all the questions you could have asked," she says, rolling off her elbow and onto her back next to me, "that is about the dumbest."

"No, really. How do you know? You've missed a period or something?"

"Yes, but I just know."

"But I mean, how can you be sure? How late are you?"

"About a month, I'd say. But Juli, I just know."

"A month isn't that late, is it? Are you usually that regular? How can you 'just know'?"

"I've been pregnant before, for one thing. I don't think I can explain how I know it, though. But I do. Let's just leave it at that."

But there hasn't been... we've hardly... I don't want to argue with her but I don't believe she could be... could know. I'm really not sure I'm ready for this.

She's up, looking at me again. "Well, what do you think about it?"

"Well, we've hardly... I don't..." I don't believe her, is what I mean. "I'm not sure it makes any difference what I think about it."

"No, I'm not sure it does. What either of us thinks. But anyway."

"If you're pregnant..."

"Not if. I am."

"All right. Since you're pregnant, I guess we'll just deal with it. Like we deal with everything else."

"It doesn't scare you?"

"I don't know if I'm scared. What about the medical... what about the birth? I guess that could be scary."

"Aside from all that. I mean about having it. Not giving birth, but us, having a child together. Bringing a child into... into this world."

"That isn't scary. Not to me. It feels, to tell you the truth, it feels kind of normal, like the next thing in line. Like the most natural thing in the world." I have to chuckle, it's so absurdly simple. Not that I really believe she is pregnant. There hasn't been enough time, has there? We haven't even made love enough, have we? Not that I think she's making it up, deliberately, to fool me. But to fool herself for some reason? Not that I trust this line of questioning. "What about you?"

"I'm scared. And I'm glad. I'm glad I told you. I'm glad you're not afraid. I'm glad you'll stay with me.

You will. Won't you?"

One time she told me she didn't want us to end up sleeping together every night. She didn't want to get into that. She might have been kidding or maybe she changed her mind. Because we do.

We usually sleep sprawled all over the bed, tangled at the knees maybe, an arm flung across the other's chest, together, but each in a separate dark place, as we were for so long, before.

But this night we are curled into each other, touching up and down our entire bodies, exhaling a musky humid atmosphere that is trapped around us by the covers, that keeps our pores open and our skins moist, as we turn together, roll into, encircle one another. Between us, safe in the hot breathy place between chins and collarbones, or protected by the overarching curve of our shoulders, or cushioned on the skimpy pillows of our two facing bellies, we cradle a space the size and texture and temperature of a purring cat, or an infant child, a live cavity, a round fleshy waiting emptiness we pass back and forth as we turn and roll and stretch and settle and hold each other, not at all awake, but not unaware either of the creaking old house and the groan of a passing great blue heron, or the dry rubbing sigh of the cabbage palms.

Juan Goytisolo
LANDSCAPES AFTER THE BATTLE

'Eloquent and profound . . . needs reading everywhere.' THE INDEPENDENT

'Juan Goytisolo is one of the most rigorous and original contemporary writers . . . *Landscapes After the Battle* [is] an unsettling, apocalyptic work, splendidly translated by Helen Lane.'
MARIO VARGAS LLOSA

'Fierce, highly unpleasant, and very funny.'
THE GUARDIAN

176 pages £7.95 (paper)

MARKS OF IDENTITY

'For me *Marks of Identity* was my first novel. It was forbidden publication in Spain. For twelve years after that everything I wrote was forbidden in Spain. So I realized that my decision to attack the Spanish language through its culture was correct. But what was most important for me was that I no longer exercised censorship on myself, I was a free writer. This search for and conquest of freedom was the most important thing to me.'

Juan Goytisolo, in an interview with CITY LIMITS

304 pages £8.95 (paper)

Janice Eidus
FAITHFUL REBECCA

'Eidus's style is witty and unpretentious, with a surrealistic edge that is never out of control. Her descriptions of Rebecca's fantasies and sensations are sensuous and erotic, with an amused awareness that her heroine, a fully paid-up member of the Me Generation, is forever trying out a succession of roles.' SUNDAY TIMES

'Funny, clever, sexy, tender and tough, a real find.'
NEW STATESMAN & SOCIETY

'A highly entertaining and refreshing book.'
THE PINK PAPER

'Moving and erotic.' TLS

176 pages £5.95